I0451768

EVEN THE RICH BEG!

EVEN THE RICH BEG!

EVEN THE RICH BEG!

Onyebuchi Obidimaru

WORDS
RHYMES &
RHYTHM

Copyright ©2018 Onyebuchi Obidimaru

ISBN: 978-978-965-581-6

All rights reserved.
No part of this book may be reproduced,
distributed, stored in a retrieval system, or
transmitted, in any form or by any means,
electronic, electrostatic, magnetic tape,
mechanical, photocopying, recording, or
otherwise without prior written permission from
the Publisher.
For information about permission to reproduce
selections from this book, write to info@wrr.ng

National Library of Nigeria Cataloguing-in-
Publication Data

Cover Design: Akila Jibrin

Printed and Published in Nigeria by:
Words Rhymes & Rhythm Limited
Suite C309, Global Plaza Plot 366, Obafemi
Awolowo Way, Jabi District, Abuja, Nigeria.
08169027757, 08060109295
www.wrr.ng

DEDICATION

To all who cared but never acted. You're the reason things turned out this way.

Chapter 1

"Hello, Miss."

Jens called out to the lady walking past him where he sat, seeking refuge from the blazing afternoon sun, under the gnarled coconut tree just beside the fence of his residence. She looked bewildered, as though she had been searching for something. It explained why she had passed without noticing his conspicuous presence.

He called out again, this time louder.

Folake heard him this time and turned her sweaty face towards him. She felt beat down. The long walk from Ajani Street, where she resided, down to Venna Street had worn her out. Worse still, she was in a neighbourhood which was very much unlike hers, with its evenly tarred, litter-free roads complete with wide drainages bordered by manicured lawns, flowers in full blossom and varieties of ornamental trees to complement the beautifully designed architecture. Everything she saw spoke affluence.

Her worry at the moment was that she'd forgotten the house number of the address she had made a mental note of. It gave her face a noticeable perplexed look. The fulgent sun didn't help matter as she felt betrayed by the patches of perspiration on her dress; showing how fried she was from inside and outside.

Since turning into Venna Street, she'd met not a single soul, at least not until the man under the coconut tree called to her.

"Good afternoon," she said when she stopped mid-stride towards him.

"What could have brought an angel like you to this street this hot afternoon?" Jens asked after nodding to her greeting. He stood up and casually assessed the hapless visitor who took a few more steps towards him. The small plastic bag she held in her right hand like that of a pilgrim in a holy land, did not provide any clue as to what her mission in the neighbourhood was.

Jens was an employee to one of the landlords in the area. It was a small neighbourhood and he prided himself in knowing almost everyone. So he knew Folake was an outsider, more likely a future employee. One thing he was certain of was that she was troubled. Her facial expression conveyed her despondency.

"Today must have been your first time on earth. Maybe I can help you with your direction if you have lost your way back to heaven," Jens quipped, chuckling at his own wittiness that seemed lost on his audience.

"Sorry sir," Folake said, wiping off sweat from her brow with her left thumb, "I'm actually looking for one Mrs. Akinyemi Folasade's house. I was told that she lives on this street but I've lost the house number and can't say which of these buildings is actually hers."

"Folasade?" Jens echoed when he heard his boss' name. He was her chauffeur. The lady nodded in the affirmative.

"Sorry oh, who are you?" he asked. His hitherto playful tone had changed into one of curiosity.

Her poorly ironed polyester gown and its many creases convinced him that she was not even close to his mistress' class as to warrant her attention. This further fuelled his sudden curiosity to know who she was.

"Please, do you know where she stays?" Folake ignored his question.

"As a matter of fact, I do. She is my Madam. So, you still haven't told me who you are...?" he paused at the question, tilting his head for emphasis

"Okay. I'm Folake and I was sent to her and I think she would be expecting me," she replied nervously as Jens' eyes remained uncomfortably fixed on her.

"Hmmm, okay. Let me go and inform her of your presence. Hope the bag is the blessings meant for us?" he teased, pointing at her plastic bag as he opened the giant gate and disappeared.

Mrs Akinyemi, a widow who worked as the internal auditor of JK Bank at its headquarters in the city, had earlier asked Jumoke, one of the bank's janitors to help her search for a charwoman after accepting the fact that she couldn't shoulder the demands of her job with her domestic work.

Jumoke, who happened to be Folake's neighbour at Ajani Street, had immediately thought of Folake who she had observed to be more often than not sitting at home idle since the university she attended, state-owned Erden Memorial University, was indefinitely shut down after students violently protested an alleged fifty percent upwards review of tuition with added charges.

Folake, faced with the options of whittling away the compulsory holiday or earning some money doing odd jobs jumped at Jumoke's offer without a second's thought. Working as a help in a high-brow neighbourhood seemed like a much better prospect than trudging along with her father to his tailoring workshop or joining her mother in vegetable trade. Neither held the promise of helping her save the extra cash she hoped to make before the school resumed, and she knew it would be a long-while giving the direction of negotiations between the students' union and the university management. Jumoke had assured her that the charwoman position would at least give her the chance to help ease the financial difficulties her parents were facing. It was no brainer. She had to take the job.

And so her she was outside the gate of her potential employer. After a few minutes wait that seemed like an eternity to her, Folake decided to go into the compound and wait by the gate to see things for herself rather than wait outside endlessly. She wondered if Jens had forgotten her.

On opening the pedestrian gate, she saw Jens dry cleaning a grey saloon car. That same moment, an extremely beautiful ebony skinned woman stepped out from the foyer of the oxblood-red painted architectural masterpiece before her.

The woman, who seemed way too young to be the person whom Jumoke had earlier described to her as 'middle-aged', was dressed in a full-length gown made from a uniquely patterned yellow Ankara fabric. Paired with matching *gele*, and luxurious accessories on her neck and wrists, she was amazing to behold. Folake was astonished.

Mrs Akinyemi noticed the young lady standing near the gate and signalled to her. She told Jens to hurry and turned to Folake who curtseyed respectfully while mumbling 'Good afternoon, ma.'

"What's that your name again?" she asked Folake ignoring her greetings.

"Folake, Folake Festus, Ma." Folake's voice quavered. She could feel her heart beating in her throat as though it would jump out. She wondered if her friend Jumoke was talking about someone else when she added "nice and easy-going" to the profile of her would-be boss.

She knew also that Mrs Akinyemi might be angry at her for coming late and resolved to explain that she was late only because she trekked the entire distance from her part of town just to save the exorbitant transport money.

Folake was right. Folasade was angry. She couldn't understand why anyone would be late on the first day of work for a job that has not been secured yet. It was unbelievable.

Even more annoying was the fact that the day was a public holiday and she'd expected that the charwoman would arrive early enough to help her with the house chores immediately. She'd initially resolved to turn her away immediately but, seeing Folake now, with her grimy face and bewildered eyes, she changed her mind.

"And I presume that you are from er..."

"Ajani Street, ma. I live in the same yard with Jumoke."

"Umm, Folake," Mrs Akinyemi called nodding her head. "Hope Jumoke told you of the work's terms before you decided to come over?"

She glanced briefly at gold-plated wristwatch and then up to face Folake who seemed to have regained her composure.

"Yes, ma." Folake answered. Jumoke had told her beforehand that the person to be employed would have had to live in the house with her and have a not-too-high wage demand.

"Are you sure? Because it seems like you are not quite ready for the job today. I don't see your things."

"I am, ma." Folake responded.

Her initial plan on leaving home was to make an appearance for the sole reason of finding out if the charwoman position was still open. She never expected to find it still available, not to be hired on the spot. It was the reason she had only two changes of clothes in her small plastic bag.

Seeing that Mrs Akinyemi expected her to take the job immediately, she quickly resolved to put a call through to her folks at home for more of her things. She threw her initial plans to ask her employer to allow her work from home out of the window. She couldn't imagine asking the stern faced lady before her for such concessions.

"With what? Or are there other belongings of yours waiting outside to be brought in?" Folasade asked, genuinely confused.

"No, ma," Folake replied. "I wanted to go and get them later or ask someone to bring them for me."

"Okay then, don't worry. Just go back and get your things ready, then come back tomorrow to start. Jens will help you get to grips with things here. I'm already late for a function and won't be in until tomorrow. So see you on Saturday."

With that, Mrs Akinyemi walked away briskly and eased herself gracefully into her idling car.

Chapter 2

"Up Nepa...!"

The children in the neighbourhood cried in excitement. They romped around.

Their joy was understandable – three months had passed since the amber-coloured electric bulbs come to life in their full radiance, without the accompanying sounds of generators. The entire area had been in darkness since unidentified vandals stole the power cables linking the community. The restoration of power was a communal effort. Some men had coordinated the collection of levies from all residents towards purchasing replacements for the stolen cables. A second round of collection, which was highly resisted, had to be done to get enough money to procure the needed materials and appease the electricity company staffs who would otherwise not come to their aid.

This blackout wasn't the first or worst of its kind in the neighbourhood. It was just another one of their tragedies. The previous year a longer spell without power was endured after hoodlums stole parts of the transformer servicing the locality and power officials, seeking to absolve themselves of complicity fingered some youths as the culprit. The ensuing blame game let to an eight-month blackout.

"*Heeei!*"

Again the neighbourhood cried out but this time, it was in disgust. Their joy had been cut short as their newly-connected electric cables crackled and gave off multi-coloured sparks that looked a lot like lightning bolts before snapping near the transformer. Darkness descended as the electric-bulbs and television sets went dead, as abruptly as they had come on. It had been barely fifteen minutes before the power was truncated.

It was time to blame someone. A very vocal resident said the power went off because of the inferior quality of the cables. Dele, the electrical appliances dealer who was a tenant in Gbaju Street, was the obvious target. He was perhaps to be blamed for this one, being part of the committee delegated to purchase the cables since Ajani Street and adjacent Gbaju Street shared the same transformer. Even before the power returned, it has been rumoured that Dele had unscrupulously procured, cheap, substandard cables which was used in fixing back the electricity and perhaps, was to blame for the blackout. A growing, disappointed crowd headed towards his dingy apartment.

Like in every home on the affected streets, the power failure left bad tempers everywhere. Oga Festus, Folake's father had turned on his eldest son Ademola as soon as the power went out.

"*Shey*, I warned you not to put on the television yet, that you should allow the light to stabilise for some time before you turn it on? But you still went ahead to do as you liked. You see now?"

Ademola had in defiance of his father's stern warning plugged in the sixteen-inch television in their parlour directly into the wall socket, despite the apparent excessive voltage that was supplied.

Had Oga Festus not quickly unplugged the TV set immediately he noticed the sparks on the cable from where he sat at the window, it would probably have been damaged like their neighbour's.

Ademola worked with his father in the tailoring workshop. They had both returned early from work that evening after completing a client's tiring work which had to be delivered the following day. The job had kept them on their feet throughout the last couple of days.

They both had had their dinner and retired to bed to get some much-needed sleep in readiness for the next day before the jubilation in the neighbourhood and crackling bulbs wiped the sleep from their eyes. Ademola had been the first to react, rolling up his mat in one quick move before heading to the parlour to charge his phone and switch the television set. Like everyone else, the return of power after such prolonged darkness was intoxicating.

"Unplug those things from the wall socket and come light this lamp in here," Oga Festus called out from the now pitch dark bedroom he had returned to after the episode with his son. The darkness was suddenly too uncomfortable. Ademola had turned off the kerosene lamp minutes before the power went out. He waited impatiently as his son carried out his orders.

Oga Festus had three children – Folake, Ademola and Badmus. Of the three, he was fondest of Ademola, who didn't seem to be as bright as his siblings. It was his apparent academic disadvantage that caused him to join his father's tailoring workshop business. Persuading Ademola to join the workshop was not easy for Oga Festus, but he persisted seeing that his son seemed more inclined towards the trade instead of continuing to claw at straws with words education.

"Ahh! Maami you are back," Ademola said when he unbolted the door to the parlour, the only passage which served as both exit and entrance to their two-room rented apartment, and waved aside the curtain, to welcome his mother who had just returned from the market with Badmus. Badmus usually helps their mother at the market after returning from school. He would help her sell her leftover wares, especially the perishable ones which would be lost to spoilage if not sold quickly.

Ademola sidestepped his sister Folake who continued sleeping on the carpeted floor of the parlour all through the ruckus caused by the short-lived power restoration. Her long trek to and from Mrs Akinyemi's residence had left her worn out. She'd only managed to serve her father and brother their share of the yam porridge she'd cooked earlier before passing out on the floor. Even her father's angry shout at Ademola had only succeeded in making her stretch and yawn.

Ademola grabbed her underarms and pulled her up to her feet. He was brutally gentle. It seemed he'd done it several times in the past. Folake didn't protest and he left her to stand on her own. He sat on the old three-seater settee in the parlour. It was burgundy when their father first bought it in over a decade ago but layers of dirt and stains of varying colours had left it rather multi-coloured. But it was still, rather surprisingly, sturdy.

"Why is our house in darkness or is it that the spark in the cable lines in Gbaju also affected us?"

"What else do you expect when the wires spark like that if not total darkness everywhere?" Badmus responded.

"Folake, didn't you go to the place you told me you needed to go to today again, Folake?" Madam Caro asked as she pulled out one plastic chair from the stack of five in one corner of the living room. She hated to sit on the settees.

"I did oh," Folake answered from the bedroom where she went to dish out the day's dinner for her mother and kid brother.

"So, what happened? You didn't get to see her or you came back home to pick some things you forgot to take along?" Madam Caro asked with concern written all over her face.

"Maami, won't you at least have your meal first?" Folake said setting a scratched stainless steel plate filled with steaming porridge on a stool before her. She went back into the bedroom and returned with another plate for Badmus.

"Is the food running away?" Madam Caro said, "Come on, tell me what happened, *joor.*"

"Since you don't want to have your food first, *oya* wait let me sit down."

Folake sat on the other sofa in the parlour. Like the burgundy settee, it had seen better days. Ademola and Badmus were seated separately in the other two battered upholsteries with their ears positioned for Folake's gist. Oga Festus was not in the parlour with them as he was in the bedroom trying to get himself to sleep early and be fresh for the next day.

"It wasn't easy locating the street Jumoke told me, not to mention of the woman's house," Folake began. She told them about the long walk, the well-groomed and beautifully-cultured area her feet took her to and how she nearly missed meeting Mrs Akinyemi. Of course she told them about her youthful elegance and the conversation they had.

"I see." Madam Caro said nodding her head. "So, from what you observed and what you saw over there, the house will treat you well, *abi*?"

"Ermm... Maami, I don't know oh." Folake replied thrusting aside her earlier acquiescence with the place.

"What do you mean by 'ermm, Maami, I don't know oh?' Was it not you that went there?"

"How can I tell? Today was just my first time there and besides I didn't even stay long there."

"Don't you know that a mature corn can easily be identified by mere looking at it?" Madam Caro said in a mellowed voice.

"Anyway, just be mindful of yourself. Such a woman as you described won't tolerate nonsense. People like her pay for efficiency and not for beauty. It will be to your advantage to be well-behaved and do your duties diligently. So be hardworking and careful in all you are tasked to do there. That's all I have to tell you for now."

With that, Mama Caro settled down to her supper which had already gone cold while they talked. She ate it without complaining. By the time she finished, Folake was already asleep with her head nested on the arm of the sofa she sat on.

Chapter 3

Jens was a man in his early-thirties but he could easily pass for a boy in his early to mid-twenties because of his youthful demeanour. He was only partially educated, having dropped out of school to go to Europe, only to be deported, hence his current employment as a chauffeur.

As he sat in the backseat of his boss' car, waiting for her to close for the day, his mind drifted to the nearly forgotten past, when he and one of his friends had decided to follow Rufus, a two-time deportee from Europe who told them that he could get them there. At the time, Jens was a fresh secondary school leaver and had only just secured admission into the university. The idea of going to Europe ate him up, especially seeing Rufus' flamboyant lifestyle, so much that neither his academic pursuit nor his father's warning and pleas could dissuade him.

"See my son, money is yet to announce when it would be leaving the world," Jens father had said on the day he broached the topic. "I wonder why you are in a hurry to have it before it leaves. Why not first be done with your education before embarking on this quest for greener pastures. Remember, the words of the elders 'that one is always counted before two, and a place where one gets to by running, another who chooses to walk will also get there'."

But none of his father's words held water, as Jens' mind was already made up. Having a one-track mind, he kept on pressing his parents for money for the trip.

Being an only son of four children, winning his father, who had always pandered to him, wasn't a hard task. Aside that, Jens had become an embarrassment to his parents, having opted to sit idle at home and aimlessly wander the streets instead of returning to the university. Jens did this deliberately, knowing that no parent would enjoy seeing their child, much less an only son, waste his life in that manner. There was also the possibility that he could succeed in his quest.

His strategy worked. Jens' parents borrowed money, using one of their landed properties as collateral, to raise the amount Rufus said would be needed to fund the trip, and support him during the first few weeks in the foreign land.

Of all those who initially showed interest in following Rufus' gateway to the '*land flowing with milk and honey,*' Jens and Deji were the only ones who were able to secure the funds on time. And that was how Jens bade farewell to his siblings, his parents and his country, utterly oblivious of what the journey entailed.

The first shock of the adventure had hit them somewhere in Zaria where Rufus handed them over to a decrepit middle-aged man simply referred to as Alhaji. The man had him twelve other people who were also interested in scooping from the same honeycomb. Six of them were ladies.

That same day they began their journey into the Sahara in a small truck covered with tarpaulin. All fourteen of them were told to sit in the back.

Alhaji sat in front with the driver. Jens soon got used to Alhaji's gruffly voice as he negotiated their way through the many checkpoints on the road.

Jens remembered the torture his feet had to endure, trekking many miles with luggage, when the truck broke down in a sea of Sahara sands with no other vehicle in sight. Alhaji had told them there was a village nearby where they would get another vehicle, but what he had not told them that 'nearby' was a two day journey, plodding through hot sand under the very harsh weather.

By midday, one of the ladies collapsed having felt spent and weary from the long walk. Jens had seen her feet wobble before she fell flat on her face. She was left behind without ceremony. Jens could swear he had seen Alhaji's driver sorting through her belonging when he turned back. The second day claimed two more people...

By the time they got to the Mediterranean and crossed over to Europe, they had been transferred between several handlers. There were only nine of them left – six males and three females. Jens and Deji were overjoyed to have made it across alive, and more importantly, together.

As newcomers with no permit work for legitimate employment, they found themselves engaged in illicit activities. The ladies quickly got into prostitution while the guys, Jens included, became drug peddlers after a two-week orientation. These socially-unacceptable jobs were the only options available to newcomers. The bosses, who provided their daily food, shelter and protection, literally owned them and were very clear about it.

A few months after their arrival, Jens and Deji were separated after the bosses dispatched them to work in different European cities. Jens found himself in Birmingham, United Kingdom and Deji in Lisbon, Portugal.

Jens thrived during the first year in Birmingham. His assigned job was distributing drugs to small-time sellers. He was even able to send some money to his parents at home. It was all good until Border Control officers nabbed him during an unannounced raid on illegal immigrants in the city. He was detained for some weeks before being deported. And that was how his dream of a beautiful life ended less than a year after he left his parents.

Jens could not return home. He knew he would be met with sneers and would be labelled the fool who gave up the bird in his hand for two in the bush. And that was how he had opted to remain in the commercial city of Goba where immigration officials released him. Brushing aside the idea of returning to school, as that implied starting all over again, he made up his mind do whatever it would take to achieve his original dream.

Jens began his new life by changing his identity. He started by shortening his name 'Jensen' to 'Jens'. He also cut his dreads and beards, both of which were part of his of signature look, in order to appear more responsible. He knew he would need it to stay afloat in Goba. The fact that appearing clean-shaven was cheaper than maintaining dreads and a full beard was an added motivation

In the months that followed, Jens did all and any work he could find to meet up with the city's demands. He obliged to do such odd jobs; worked at a car wash, loaded goods at factories, and he even had a brief stint as a bartender. These odd jobs certainly didn't make it rain as he would have loved, but his bills were paid.

In his fourth month, which happened to be the second year since he left home for Europe, Jens applied for a security position at JK Bank. He and three others were selected out of the hundreds of applicants. It was there that he met Mrs Akinyemi, who eventually offered to house and employ him as her chauffeur. She would later tell him that she employed him for his smart appearance and pleasant manners.

Working in Mrs Akinyemi's household eventually chiselled away his rough edges. With her constant words of encouragement, his perspective of life changed. He had hope again. It was that hope that had kept him pushing.

Working with a recently widowed woman with two kids wasn't all rosy though, especially when she had her mood swings. He doubled as chauffeur and house help but the pay was very good. He was treated like a member of the family and given a room inside the house. He lived inside the house which, according to Mrs. Akinyemi, was personally designed by her late husband such that there was a room apiece for himself, his wife, his kids and any guest that had to stick around for a while. Jens pondered the irony of the fact that it was he himself, Mr. Akinyemi, who eventually didn't stick around long enough to fully enjoy the luxurious life he had intended for both himself and his family, falling victim to death's cold hands shortly after finishing it.

Mr. Akinyemi's sudden demise had so distressed his wife that she was hospitalized shortly after his burial. Despite her elegance and colourful demeanour, Jens, who knew her before her loss, could tell that a part of her was still missing, maybe gone forever.

Maybe that was part of why he welcomed the idea of Folake coming into his boss' household. It would certainly mean less stress on her, more order and efficiency around the mammoth five-bedroom duplex. It had long been obvious that more hands were needed to keep the house in shape.

Chapter 4

People grieve differently. When her husband died, Folasade threw herself into her work, totally, as a way of getting over it. It landed her into the hospital at first. But it soon became normal. She worked as though she owed her husband a debt and would have to work for eternity to be able to repay.

As a wife and mother, Folasade's utmost desire was to uphold his legacy of securing the best possible life for herself and their kids. She worked at this mission every waking hour. Her hard work and diligence didn't go unnoticed at the bank and she was soon showered with promotions which launched her into the upper echelons of the banking sector.

This progress had its own problems. Combining work commitments with mummy duties without a live-in help often left her playing catch up. She struggled to keep up with the demands. It was this very fact that led to the hiring on Jens.

Driving home one evening, after a particularly gruelling day, she had drifted into the subconscious and momentarily lost control of her vehicle. Only a last minute decision to swerve hard to the right saved her the head-on collision that would have turned her kids into orphans. On the advice of her pastor and doctor, she poached Jens from the bank and stopped driving altogether the following week. She also became more regular at church, avoided lonely places as this was where she was likely to be melancholic. Her doctor was particular about getting extra hands at home for the sake of her health.

Having Jens in the house helped a lot, but it wasn't enough. He was overwhelmed with the tasks, especially when the children were away at boarding school. Besides his chauffeuring duty, Jens cared for the house, dropping off and picking up dirty laundry at laundry services, shopping and serving as substitute chef whenever Mrs. Folasade was stressed, depressed or otherwise engaged, which was often in the beginning. Folake's coming would change that.

So far, Folake had proven efficient. She saw to it that the house was always kept in pristine condition and meals were cooked and served in time.

***

"Mummy! Mummy!"

Ten-year-old Damilola called out as she bumbled into the kitchen. Folake, who was initially startled, had a delightful smile on her face. It was the younger girl's turn to be startled.

"Good afternoon?" Damilola blurted when she realized the person in the kitchen wasn't her mother. She bounded out of the kitchen immediately. Jens had just picked her and her brother from school for a week-long break.

Damilola ran up the stairs to her brother's room. She met him unpacking his PlayStation video game console from where he had stashed it before leaving for school at the beginning of the term.

Olumide noticed his sister's countenance immediately she stepped into the room.

"What's wrong with you?" he asked.

"Mom's not home."

"Really? So who is in the kitchen? I heard noise from there."

"There's a young woman there. I don't know who she is. I was surprised when I saw her. So I simply greeted her and left."

"Have you asked Uncle Jens who she is?" Olumide asked, obviously disinterested. He was untangling the cords of his gaming pads. All he wanted to do them was set up his game and have fun.

"Let's go together," Damilola suggested. Olumide obliged, albeit reluctantly. But Jens was nowhere to be found in the building and the car was not in the compound either. They went back into the house and met the stranger in the living room, smiling at them.

"Dami, Olumide, why not go in, have a change of clothes and then come over for lunch?"

"She already knows our names?" Damilola mumbled to herself.

Even Olumide, who didn't hear his sister, seemed visibly flustered that Folake knew their names. But her request seemed polite and harmless and so they obliged. They were hungry as well. So the idea of lunch sounded like music to their ears. The aroma wafting into their nostrils convinced them.

Lunch was pasta garnished with steamed veggies and fish sauce. Folake introduced herself to the kids as she served them generous portions. They relaxed almost immediately and immediately got down to devouring the delicious meal.

By the time the rest of the family arrived, Folake and the kids were best buddies. They took quite a liking to her and Folake on her own part grew very fond of them, transforming into a 'big sister figure'.

She helped them with their school assignments and they in turn spared their playtime to help her with some chores – which was unbelievable for Mrs Akinyemi, especially when she noticed that Olumide took time off his gaming to keep her company. She was very much pleased to find Damilola, her daughter, was finally getting interested in the kitchen. That was unthinkable not so long ago.

Her children's new-found enthusiasm for domestic chores within that one week pleased her beyond words. The holiday turned out to be a blessing for them all. It was no wonder the kids were visibly sad that Sunday evening when Jens announced it was time to return to school.

Chapter 5

The experience Folake garnered during her brief employment as a cook's assistant in a restaurant before gaining admission into Erden Memorial University put her in rather good stead for the job she was expected to do as Mrs. Folashade's live-in help.

She cooked with such skill that there was never talk of too much or too little of any cooking ingredient in her meals, and it was often difficult to decide which was better between the look, aroma or taste of whatever she prepared. The house itself wore a new look under her care. Nothing ever seemed to be out of its place with her in the house.

Folake also proved very much handy with laundry, so much that the laundry man commented about the significant drop in his dues from Mrs. Folasade's household to Jens. She did most of the household's laundry except for the occasional few that Mrs. Folashade insisted on sending to the laundry man.

"Have you seen today's papers?" Jens asked as he entered the kitchen that evening to make small talk with Folake, who was cooking dinner.

Jens loved to talk with Folake, who was mostly by herself in the building during the day. He had three newspapers with him.

"What's new?" Folake asked without turning to look at him. She turned off the gas cooker and stirred the pot of *ewedu* soup that was almost boiling over on it. "The normal political propagandas to win the empathy of unsuspecting citizens, or is it about the recent flood that ravaged of the market?"

"No. There's that and more. Very different."

"Well, tell me about it".

"Why not see for yourself," Jens said, holding out the newspapers.

The first paper had an ugly picture of the recently flooded Agbaja central market. According to the paper, the disaster was attributed to the blockage of the market's drainage system and had turned the market into a mini river, rendering some shops and their contents useless.

The traders were partly to blame. In spite of campaigns and numerous sensitizations organized by the government against the indiscriminate dumping of refuse, and the provision of waste bins, incinerators, most traders continued to dump their waste into the gutters and canals. It was this act that led to the clogging of the sewage system and the resultant flood.

Three headlines caught Folake's attention in the papers:

"Academic activities resumes again in Erden Memorial University after four months...."
"Erden Memorial University conditionally recalls her students back to classes...."
"Erden Memorial University makes an unusual offer to students of the institution..."

Folake was left bemused by the Erden University stories. The school authorities had mandated students to pay the proposed reviewed fees and an additional fifteen percent of the said amount as fine for the damages caused to school property during the riot if they wished to continue their studies. The articles made it clear that the state government backed the decision.

According to the school authorities, some of the school's most valuable assets had either been vandalized or destroyed while some equipment in the school's science lab and ICT centre were carted away. The fifteen percent surcharge was intended for repairs and replacements. All students were expected to comply or risk forfeiting their studentship. To ensure compliance, the university directed that all students must register their semester courses with a receipt indicating payment.

The news left Folake disheartened. She had long anticipated the news of resumption. It hadn't occurred to her that such conditions would come with it.

She had to do something fast. She knew that having been closed for four months closure, lectures and exams would be rushed to keep pace with the national academic calendar. The few friends she talked to had mixed feelings about the resumption. The ones who were unoccupied during the compulsory holiday were eager to resume while those who were engaged like her even wished for an extension.

Folake made up her mind to continue her services at the Akinyemi's while pursuing her academic degree. First she had to deal with the issue of the surcharge. She did not have enough to cover for fess and surcharge. She dialled her mother's number.

Folake earned her mother's praise for her decisive courage when she announced her decision to keep her employment and study at the same time. But when she brought up the issue of finance, Madam Caro sighed deeply.

"Business hasn't been as good as it used to be. The flood, that flood finished me," she said. "And your father has been complaining a lot lately of low turnout of customers in his workshop. Last week he borrowed money from me for Badmus's fees."

"My monthly salary I was sending home *nko*?"

"That's what I'm saying, that it has been used in taking care of the family's needs. You know I don't spend money uselessly."

"So what do you want me to do now? Quit school or …"

'The line went dead. Folake checked her airtime and realized it was exhausted. She borrowed airtime from her network provider and dialled back. She wanted her mother to explain what she implied by her response. She couldn't believe that all her earnings could be spent without consulting her or considering her own welfare.

She tried redialling her mother's number several times but the network was poor as usual. At her thousandth attempt, the line connected.

"Hello! Maami, how come nobody thought about me and my own school fees?"

"I'm sorry my daughter, but we didn't know it would turn up like this...the flood and your school calling off the closure were unexpected."

Folake softened at her mother's tone.

"Why not look for where to borrow money? When I get paid, you can then proceed with paying back the money," she suggested.

"I have actually thought about that but we have a terrible credit history. You know your daddy is a bad debtor. He's notorious for defaulting when it comes to repaying debts."

Folake sighed. Everyone knew her father and his debt issues, "So what am I going to do, Maami?"

"Ehm...," Madam Caro paused for a moment, "have you considered asking your Madam for help? How about you plead with her to pay you for like four months upfront to settle your fees in school?"

"Hmm! You think it's a good idea? I have not even told her I want to return to school yet."

"Just ask her first and then get back to me. You know, there's nothing wrong in at least trying. And again, please, try to be open with your mistress in your dealings with her."

"I've heard you, Maami. Let's just hope she grants my request. If not, you and daddy will have to come up with something oh."

Folake was reluctant at first to go to Auntie Sade – as Mrs Akinyemi preferred to be addressed by her employees, outside the office.

She first sought Jens' counsel. In his usual lively manner, he allayed her fears away and advised her to go about it in a manner as polite as she could muster. She knew there was no other way around it other than presenting her request to Auntie Sade, one way or another.

It turned out that Folake's fears were unfounded. Folasade was more than willing to help her with her predicament. She willingly accepted both the idea of studying while working for her and the upfront payment of wages to deal with the school fees issue.

To Folasade, Folake had become a very important part of her family and helping her was like helping her kids. She even offered some advice to the younger woman on how she could successfully combine her academic activities with her duties.

Chapter 6

Life at the Akinyemis' certainly came with its merits but it took its toll on Folake's academics. As is the case with almost every good thing, the new lease of life that she had obtained came at a price and it was her grades that took the hardest hit.

Before her employment at the Akinyemis, she had an enviable grade point average of 3.90, and she had hoped to build on it. Juggling both school and work had proven to be more difficult than anticipated as evidenced by the results of the first two semesters she had gone through while working in the household. For the first time, Folake failed two courses. She experienced the shame of having to deal with 'carry-overs'.

The saddest thing about her failure was that she had remained punctual to classes, attended all lectures and worked hard at her assignments and tests. Oftentimes, she would cram as much as she could the day before exams or tests.

At the end of it all, the results on the notice board would only mock her efforts. Folake knew it was all due to her inability to find enough study time. The after-school chores that she had to take care of all by herself often left her too spent to study.

But it had not been all doom and gloom for Folake. Indeed, her fortunes had changed for the better and this was visible in her appearance. Her skin glowed and she looked alive. She now ate well, being the one in charge of the kitchen, and no longer had to experience the stress of public transport or walking all the way to school as Jens drove her everywhere on Mrs Akinyemi's orders. She no longer had to trudge long distances to get clean water because, with a borehole installed in Auntie Sade's house, clean water was always available.

Money was also no longer a problem. Her boss ensured that her monthly pay and other allowances were paid in time. Her room, much unlike the one she shared with her siblings back home, was tastefully furnished and well-ventilated with a bathroom en suite.

Folake knew she had a lot to be grateful for. This was why she couldn't complain about the stress she now had to deal with as a working student.

In an attempt to show gratitude for the much-improved lifestyle she now lived, thanks in no small part to Mrs Akinyemi's unexpected benevolence, she had promised herself to never be found wanting.

She made it her unwritten rule to get up as early as the wee hours of the morning to get breakfast ready. Sometimes she would prepare lunch as well. She would do these while putting the house in order. By 7:30 a.m., Jens who would have returned from dropping off Mrs. Akinyemi would drive her to the university campus.

Jens would return by 4:30 p.m. to bring her back home to prepare dinner which had to be served by 7:00 p.m. After eating dinner together with Mrs.

Akinyemi, she would spend a few more hours dealing with more chores preparing for the following day. It was a tiring pattern that often saw her retiring late to bed and getting up really early every other day.

Folake was definitely not a favourite in the reckoning of most of her male course mates. As a matter of fact, most of them avoided her, and it wasn't had little to with her looks or brains, because she was very beautiful and is regarded as intelligent by those who knew her well. Her sin was her reserved attitude, often distracted demeanour and noticeably formal interaction. She kept a lot to herself and made it obvious she wasn't big on making many friends, especially male ones. This earned her the 'lone wolf' label and a few snide remarks. At some point, there were gossips about her being queer, spread by spurned male admirers who couldn't understand why a beautiful woman like here would be so offish.

When Folake first learnt of her colleague's opinion of her, she was saddened; not because of the stereotypes and labels, but for the fact that no one had actually ever asked her directly why she often kept to herself and acted differently. Even though she wouldn't willingly divulge any information about herself to them, she would have at least appreciated the respect. Instead they were slapping her with inappropriate labels, even though they knew very little about her.

She often wondered if any of the many male admirers she had turned down would treat her differently had she told him that she was still suffering from the psychological trauma of being a rape victim in a society that judged her more than her assailant.

That experience had shaped her present opinion of men, but her decision to shut them all out was borne of the stories she had heard of the lasciviousness of the male folk. She wasn't ready to deal with the drama and inevitable emotional trauma that ultimately crowned such romantic relationship. To her, men were the worst and she needed to keep them at arm's length for the sake of her sanity.

It had been almost three years since the unfortunate rape incident, but Folake's emotional nerves were still as shocked as they were the day it happened. That day, Folake was on her way to the market in the wee hours of the morning, carrying a heavy bundle of wares that her mum would sell that day. She had to leave that early because it was the only way her mum, who had no stall of her own, would be able to secure a good spot to sell her wares. It had become her job, since graduating from high-school, to move her mother's wares to the market and hold the spot until her arrival much later in the morning.

On that day, Folake had taken a short-cut that her mother, were she there with her, would never have allowed her to. It was a narrow path that connected their neighbourhood to the market quickly, but it was notorious for all kinds of vices. No single day passed without someone suffering a misfortune on that route. The lucky victims lost only bags and phones. Others, especially women and girls, suffered greater misfortunes. Though the local vigilante group manned the area very often, it had never been truly rid of miscreants.

But that day, having woken up later than usual and fearing that her mother's favourite spot could be occupied by someone else, she took the shortcut praying that nothing would happen to her. Folake walked swiftly. She was afraid. Her heart pounded so loudly that its fast paced *thump thump* was all she could hear. She was halfway through when a man armed with a dagger appeared before her out of the shadows. She had turned to flee but ran into another assailant who immediately gagged her with a stinking handkerchief as the basket on her head fell over.

The men dragged her to a dark corner of the road and took turns forcing themselves on her. When they were done, they took off with her phone.

She had remained there, battered, bruised and hurt. Hot tears ran down her cheeks. She was confused, wondering if she should remain on the same spot and attract sympathizers, go back home and tell her parents what happened, or to get back up on her feet, find the basket containing her mom's wares and continue on her way to the market.

She knew people would blame her for taking the path at that time of day, knowing the dark stories that had been told about it. She also knew that people would always see her as a rape victim, just like her friend who was raped by armed robbers in her parent's home. People still insulted her with the ordeal.

Folake concluded it would be better to avoid the ignominy and stigma that would follow if word ever got out about her violation. She resolved to keep the incident to herself and take it to her grave if she had to. Having made her mind up, she got back on her feet and dusted herself up. She found her basket, gathered what was left of her mother's wares and trudged on to the market.

She was a different person.

Chapter 7

"You can only lure people by offering them what they need and not what they already have or can easily get for themselves," Folasade said to Yetunde. They were chatting in her living room. It was a Saturday.

"What do you mean exactly?" Yetunde asked. Yetunde, JK Bank's Chief Financial Officer is Folasade's colleague and long-time ally. She was in the neighbourhood to visit a family member and decided to drop by her friend's house.

"You see ehh..." Folasade continued, picking up her nearly empty glass of wine. She took a sip and returned it to its place on the side stool. "He offered me a sort of blank cheque and granted me a car loan."

"Lucky you, I must say, Sade."

"The most striking thing was that he approved my medical vacation straightaway. I know it's kind of obligatory but giving me the nod at that instant, without demanding the mandatory paperwork, is amazing."

"You see, that's what I'm saying. Kehinde is ready to do even more if you cover for him."

"Cover for him?"

"Yes, to make him do more."

"No. It seems you don't get me. Those things, everything he's offering, I can readily get for myself if I ever needed to."

"Huh?"

"Yes." Folasade said with a nod. "It is obvious that he is and has been good to me. But giving in to his demands and accepting his advances is a no-no for me. How can I rip people off just to please him? Please!"

"Ahh! Sade, come on, what's wrong with you?"

They were talking about their boss Kehinde Olufade, JK Bank's Chief Operating Officer. Kehinde had found himself in big trouble at the bank after taking a huge loan to fund a power generating set distribution company. As COO, Kehinde secured the loan at an interest rate far lower than what was normally obtainable. He had intended to explore his entrepreneurial skills by capitalising on the government's failure to provide stable electricity to the general public. He had intended the business as his retirement plan, but fate would not have it so.

His shipment of power generating sets was lost to the ravages of sea. Having paid only for minimal insurance cover in a bid to cut costs, he was left with a huge debt. So, in order to cover for his misfortune, he had approached the heads of the bank's accounting department with a shady deal that will see them expunge all records of the transaction and keep his nose clean.

He proposed a brilliant scheme that would see him pay nothing. According to his plan, the loan would be repaid with systematic deductions from the bank's monthly revenue. In return for their cooperation, he promised to give everyone a handsome cut from the insurance payout for the ill-fated shipment.

The plan was watertight but Folasade would have none of it. As the internal auditor, she had insisted that Kehinde should either take full responsibility for the loan and repay every dime, or ask for an extension that will enable him do so.

After several unsuccessful moves to get Folasade to subscribe to his plan, the COO decided to deploy Yetunde, who had already gotten some hush money, a means to get her.

"See, he is lucky that I haven't reported him already and that is simply because a part of me sympathizes with him. But, *ore mi*, he can't have everyone pay for his misfortune," Folasade said with a look of resolution on her face.

"Sade, listen, it's one request. Just this one request that COO is asking from us, from me, from you. That's all," Yetunde insisted. Even as she talked, she knew her friend would not sanction the arrangement and then it would backfire.

"Madam," Folasade said in a tone she reserved for angry moments, "I won't be part of it. I always stay above board and play by the books. Had he asked for a loan extension, I would have considered it but he is asking for an illegal easy way out. He wants outright dismissal of a loan he's already taken, at the expense of other people's investments? Sorry to disappoint you but I'll play no part in this because it goes against everything I believe in."

"How can you be so mean to him? Has he ever hurt or disappointed you in the past? Even if that is the case, you can let go, can't you?" Yetunde replied in desperation.

"Hehehe," Folasade chuckled. *"Haba!* Not at all my dear, I'm only trying to keep the record books straight, that's all. I'm doing it for all of us, to save our jobs. Are you not concerned about the bank's future?"

Yetunde did not reply.

"Well, if you are not, I am," Folasade continued. "See, I am the highest-ranking officer after the COO and may likely succeed him whenever his tenure expires or whenever he decides to step down from his position. What would be my fate if this deal you're so much in support of plunges the bank into a financial quagmire by then?"

"Sade, you never cease to amuse me with your ambitions," Yetunde could barely veil her anger.

"Call it anything you wish. I've made my stand known to you and I would not be shifting grounds on the matter."

"Don't be a sell-out, Sade. You're only trying to get in the way of someone else's happiness and peace of mind. And it's not like any of it was really his fault."

Yetunde stood up, grabbed her handbag and headed for the door. She felt deflated, wondering if she had made the proposition at the wrong time or certainly, the wrong place.

"Mind you," Folasade replied, "I should be the one calling you a sell-out for agreeing to short-change people who entrusted their wealth into your hands. That's unethical, you know!"

Folasade emptied her glass and got up to see her angry friend off.

"Since Kehinde has already succeeded in getting you to play dirty, I might just suspend my medical to see the end of this."

***

The following Monday, Folasade took charge of the entire bank like a conquering general. She started by directing all staff to straighten all their records immediately. Her directives and instructions were respected by every member of staff, including the COO.

A few days later, Henry, the bank's loan officer, entered her office with a big smile on his face. Folasade reciprocated with a smile that quickly became a frown as he stated his mission. He was there on Kehinde's request. She concluded that Henry had been fed the same fodder as Yetunde.

"I don't know why you people can't understand that we are running a financial institution and not a charitable organization. Even if it were a charitable organization, we can't just sit back, fold our hands and watch the COO plunge it into financial ruins with no regard for the resources invested in its operations," Folasade said, struggling to keep her voice down.

As if on cue, Kehinde barged into her office.

"Help me do this, I beg you," he was almost in tears. "I promise to be careful and more prayerful next time."

Folasade switched her gaze from Henry to Kehinde. She was disgusted.

"Sir, it's not that I'm trying to harm you, but the right thing has to be done."

"Forget the right thing, Sade. Just help me."

"Sir, what you are asking of me is very much against the ethics of our profession. If you so insist, how then would the discrepancy in our bottom lines and drop in profits be explained?"

"Please, you need not worry about that. Leave that to me. It will be my headache to take care of those details. See..." Kehinde sat down to face Folasade who had not gotten out of her seat all the while. "We are going to put up a kind of smokescreen and attribute the drop in revenue to the expenditures we had to deal with during the establishment of our two new branches at Ileka Housing Estate and Agbaja Central Market. We could also throw in the increased tax rates and other miscellaneous expenses incurred by the bank for good measure. No one would do as much as bat an eyelid."

He laid his plans out without stuttering or pausing for a moment's thought. Just as Folasade suspected, he had thought out the plan very carefully, and sold it to his cohorts so many times that it now came naturally.

"Again, what we present to the board is what they'll take," Henry added.

"Hmm, Interesting!" That was all Folasade could muster. She asked for time to consider the proposition. Kehinde and Henry left feeling she was all but convinced, but Folasade was far from convinced.

Her thoughts on the proposition turned up double-sided. Giving the green light to the proposal would make her colleagues happy but she was also worried about the ethical implications. She was also worried that it might come back to haunt them all in the not-so-distant future.

A sharp pain cut through her at that instant. It was very brief but it left her heart heavy and pounding out of control. She decided there and then that the COO's proposal would have to wait until her return from her medical leave.

Chapter 8

Folasade's decision to proceed on her leave at the time was entirely to enable her have her routine medical check-up and put her mind and body in good shape. She would need a sound body and mind for JK Bank's executive board and annual shareholders meetings, both of which would hold in less than three months.

As she prepared for her trip to the United Kingdom where she had an appointment with a cardiologist recommended by her Nigerian doctor, Folasade informed her staff that they could take the time off until her return. It would be a long break, the longest yet for Folake who had never been away from the house for more than three nights at a time since taking up employment there.

Folake was welcomed home by four hours of uninterrupted power supply on the evening of her return to what was quickly becoming unfamiliar surroundings. It was indeed a wonder to have power for so long in the neighbourhood. She had expected to meet the blackout she left the last time she was around.

When the power was finally cut the following morning after its usual on-and-off syndrome, she took a bucket and went to fetch water for a bath. After fetching water from the well behind the house, she made her way to the public bathrooms with a bath towel wrapped around her midriff, the bucket of water in one hand and a small plastic bowl, which held bathing soap and sponge, in the other. There were two cubicles and both were empty.

"Ahh! Folake, you're home. When did you return?" Someone called to her.

Folake dropped her bucketful of water and turned to see who it was. A fair-skinned lady stepped into view from behind a cluster of mature banana suckers. Folake could not recognize her and initially concluded she must be a member of the new family of six whom her mother had said recently moved into Mr. Femi's former two-bedroom apartment. She wondered how the lady knew her name and spoke with a hint of familiarity.

"Who is this *Oyibo* that knows my name *oh*?" Folake said. As the lady approached, the face gradually grew familiar. "Jesus! Jumoke! It is you!"

"Yes o!"

"What happened to your skin? How did you get so light?" Folake was genuinely perplexed. She placed the soap bowl in the bucket of water.

"*Ahnahn*, calm down. Why are you shouting like that? Bush girl, *you never change ehh...*?" Jumoke reprimanded her neighbour playfully.

"But eh...

"Don't *but* me *abeg*," Jumoke said. "Why are you trying to embarrass me this morning? Please go and have your bath before someone else gets into the good bathroom before you. We can talk afterwards."

Jumoke had expected that Folake's new found life at Mrs Akinyemi's place, which was in a buzzing district and her exposure to the nuances of campus life would have at least acquainted her with fashion and beauty trends, of which skin-toning was one of them. It annoyed her that her friend had experienced no such refinement. To her, Folake would never be rid of the mentality of squalor. It seemed she was born for the inner city life with its uneven roads, overflowing drainages, poor sewage disposal, absence of portable water and a general lack of basic amenities.

Jumoke, a spinster in her mid-thirties, considered her present neighbourhood beneath her. She lived with the hope of marrying into an affluent family someday. Unfortunately, she had no luck when it came to relationship, being unable to keep any for more than a few weeks. Being unmarried at her age, despite her good character and looks was a major source of worry. It was this worry that motivated her to try the skin lightening procedure in order to be more attractive.

Later that morning, she told Folake that she had quit her janitorial position at JK Bank to be able to commit more time to her new relationship with the latest love of her life, Kayode. Though Folake didn't seem to think it was a good idea to surrender her source of income but Jumoke was determined to do her best to make the relationship grow into marriage as quickly as possible.

***

Folake was hardly ever at home during the two-week break as she was always hanging out with some friends. It was all she could do to endure the boredom. Mrs Akinyemi's medical trip had come two weeks into Erden Memorial University's end of session break. So she had nothing to do.

One evening, two days before her scheduled return to her mistress's house, Folake told her mother about her falling grades.

"Maami, I would like to stop working in that house," she said.

"Ahh!" Her mother exclaimed. She choked as she struggled to swallow her mouthful of beans porridge and talk at the same time. Folake gave her a cup of water which she emptied in a hurry and handed the cup back to her.

"Ehen, what were you talking about?"

"I said I want to quit my job at Auntie Sade's house."

"Why?" Her mother queried. "Is it now that we're feeling the impact of your stay there that you want to stop? Hmm, my daughter, I won't lie to you, we all depend on your pay over there to survive these days because business has been moving from bad to worse for both me and your father. There isn't much we can do to help you or your siblings at this point in time. My trade is only able to put food on the table, with nothing left for other expenses."

"Maami," Folake sighed deeply. She wanted to tell her mother of her sleepless night and her falling grades. But the look of resignation on her mother's face muted her.

"We only depend on your pay for all these other expenses. I get up in the morning, have my bath and take my wares to the market, only to return in the evening with nothing to show for the hours spent under the sun and even in the rain. Those big shops have snatched all our customers. Buyers now prefer to shop in comfortable environments than put up with the dirty market that is crawling with criminals."

"But Maami," Folake interrupted, finding her voice at last. "I might be unable to graduate with a good grade if I continue to live and work in that house. I rarely have any time for my books there."

"It that all, or is there something you're not telling me? If you have done anything wrong to your madam, feel free to tell me now, because it's only when the hen farts that it runs around to escape the wrath of the land," Madam Caro said glaring at her daughter. "Don't you know that you are a woman and besides? Who cares about grades these days? Or do you think men marry grades?"

Her mother's words stung more than the pains of seeing her grades fall every semester. She quietly sat up and left the living room. She was boiling with anger.

"You people should have told me that I should go to school and watch others *nah*. After all, a man will always be there to take me to his house, *abi*?" Folake later screamed from the bedroom where she had retreated to calm down.

She had not expected such disappointing words from her mother.

"If you like, go there and misbehave. That's your own cup of tea. Just graduate and bring home a man that will take care of us and your siblings, that's all," Madam Caro continued.

"You should have kept me at home, then. Why send me to school if your plan for me all along was to marry me off to some man?" Folake shouted back.

Her mother's words had really upset her. She wondered how her own mother could be encouraging her to sacrifice her academics.

Folake was certain that the outcome would have been different if her father were around when she brought up the issue. He would have thought of another way of getting her relieved of the burden she so prematurely bore. But her father was away at their village for a clan meeting and would be away for two more days.

Her brothers, who would probably have been able to make their mother see reason, were also away that evening, probably watching a live soccer game in one of the public viewing centres in the neighbourhood.

It was sadly ironic that Folake had told her mother first, trusting that she would see things from her perspective and accede to her plans.

How wrong she was. It hurt her deeply.

She was still crying when Jens called to tell her that Mrs Akinyemi had informed him of her return. He said he was already on the way to pick her from the airport and Folake should cancel her plans for the next morning and return to the house.

She was more than willing to oblige.

Chapter 9

While Folasade way away, Kehinde had made moves towards getting himself out of his financial troubles. As a dogged individual, he had always found a way to meander out of the tightest spots, and it was this same trait that had aided him up the rungs of the corporate ladder. The bank's board had taken this into consideration when approving his nomination and subsequent appointment as the bank's COO.

Kehinde had a two-edged approach. One side was feigned weakness in the face of opposition. The other caused damage behind the scene. He was a master of this art of deceitful diplomacy. Where it failed to achieve his desired results, he was not afraid of taking even more dangerous measures.

Having been unable to convince Mrs Akinyemi to play ball, he had concluded that he would have to take her out of the game altogether. In furtherance of this eventuality, he recruited some hands and planted them in different strategic positions. Yetunde, Folasade's most trusted friend, was billed to play the lead role in this conspiracy, inadvertently aided by her medical trip.

The COO's grand plan was to prepare two different reports for the bank's annual fiscal year. One would contain the necessary phony deductions and the other was to be the original report without shady padding, just as Folasade wanted it. He had already managed to get the management's approval to make the annual shareholders' meeting earlier than usual. This move, he hoped, would give Folasade very little time to have a thorough read of the entire report.

Kehinde was determined to go any length to save his skin even though it meant throwing her under the bus. He would orchestrate accusations that could see her indicted for conspiracy to defraud the bank. There was also a plan to use her recent trip against her. It would be casually suggested that she had left the country briefly to finalize shady deals with her co-conspirators.

***

Kehinde rolled out his plan upon Folasade's return. His cohorts played it cool around her while the COO continued to feign submission and meekness towards her. Acting her part, Yetunde offered to help Folasade with her paperwork. Perceiving no foul play, Folasade accepted.

A fortnight two before the bank's board meeting, Yetunde left two copies of the annual report with identical covers at Folasade's desk. One was doctored as planned.

Folasade, weary from the night vigil she attended the night before, casually flipped through one report and appended her signature to both copies. Yetunde returned to grab 'their own' copies and went over to the COO's office.

***

On the day of the scheduled executive board meeting, with every preparation *okayed*, Folasade deliberately arrived late to avoid having to speak with the COO. Wearing a neatly pressed, stone-black suit over a sleeved, sky-blue shirt and a black, French heel shoe to match, she strutted her way into the bank's conference room for the meeting. She didn't detour to her office as was her tradition on such days.

The smile she wore on her face when she walked into the room did a better job of exchanging pleasantries than the hugs and words she exchanged with her colleagues and some of the board members who were already seated and waiting for the meeting to begin.

Kehinde hugged her with a sly grin on his face before shaking her hand. His heart had momentarily skipped a beat when she walked into the hall. He had never experienced such trepidation all his life. Perhaps it was due to the terrifying nightmare he had two nights back. He had beaten his dog to death in the dream for vomiting on him.

Few minutes into the meeting, Kehinde whispered into Folasade's ear to meet him for a quick talk in his office. He was visibly flustered as he got up and walked out. Her presence in the room tormented him. He had earnestly prayed that she would be absent from the day's meeting, perhaps, due to some illness or the other. Sitting beside her felt like hiding a hot potato inside the mouth.

Folasade noticed his unease and decided to accept his request and asked Yetunde to accompany her. Yetunde was totally oblivious of the COO's state of mind.

They found Kehinde seated with his hand folded on his desk. He was fidgeting nervously and gazed blankly at them.

"What is the matter, sir? Is there a problem?" Folasade was the first to find her voice.

"Ermm, nothing. Just a little issue."

"What is it, sir? Is it something we can help you with?"

"To a great extent, yes."

"So, what's it then?" Folasade asked him again.

"Sade, eh..."Kehinde began, exhaling heavily. He was still unsure of how she would react if he opened up and bared the whole issue to her. "Don't be offended by what you'll see or hear in there in the day's meeting."

"What do you mean by that, sir?" Folasade asked, having noticed that rather than swivel between the two women present, his gaze was fixated on her.

"See eh, the documents to be presented in there are not what you think they are. We doctored them. They were fabricated," Kehinde continued.

"Sorry, I'm not sure I follow. Are you trying to say that the documents we are to present today are not what they should be?" Folasade asked incredulously.

Kehinde supplied a nod implying that he wasn't bluffing.

"Doctored by whom?"

"Us actually..." Kehinde's voice had become hoarse.

"Yetunde, you are also aware of this. Aren't you?" Folasade turned her attention to her friend.

"Yes. You left us with no option," Yetunde answered defiantly, nodding her head.

"Shut up!" Folasade roared uncharacteristically."Devil and his cohort, I left you with no option indeed. You manipulated it, kept me out of it, and brought me in here hush me, *abi*? You think it's going to work that easily?"

Just then, a knock was heard on the door to inform them of the arrival of JK Bank's Chairman and CEO, dousing the tension in the office. Kehinde got up from where he was seated, checked himself to make sure nothing was out of place, in readiness to receive the Chairman.

"Please, Folasade, don't dwell on this. We will get to talk more after the meeting, or..."Kehinde patted Folasade on her shoulder. He felt relieved, having successfully transferred his distress to her. His lips were however pressed against each other as he left the office, closing the door behind the two women who stood motionless.

Folasade was shocked by her own naivety. She couldn't believe they got her to sign false documents. They had obviously succeeded in pulling a fast one on her despite her resistance. As she walked back to the hall with her hands clasped behind, her mind was restless. She suddenly felt lightheaded as she entered.

Five minutes later, the Chairman entered the conference room, laughing loudly over something

Kehinde had said. They met a mild commotion. Everyone in the room seemed confused and pointing at something. Kehinde saw a motionless body on the marble floor and knew instantly who it was. Only one person had that suit.

His heart skipped a thousand beats.

Chapter 10

The day seemed to drag on forever for Folake who was alone. She waited for Mrs. Akinyemi's return for hours on end on the veranda, braving the cold night with only a light T-shirt. Every sound that resembled a moving vehicle interested her. But it was a fruitless wait and she left the veranda for the comfort of the living room around 8 p.m. She wondered why she couldn't reach both Jens and their boss on phone.

There entire house was dimly lit by a single rechargeable lamp because the power was out in the estate and Jens wasn't home to turn on the generator. The darkness and the cold night combined to make Folake very alone and lonely. She was hungry, but was unable to eat, worried about the night that seemed odd. It was unusual that both Jens and Mrs. Akinyemi would turn off their phones at the same time.

Folake tried her best to keep her eyelids open, but soon lost the battle. She curled up in the sofa and snored to her heart's content. She was so deep in sleep that she did not notice when the front door opened and someone walked in.

"Folake, Folake."

It was Jens. He tapped Folake's shoulder to rouse her from sleep. Half awake, Folake gave him an empty stare. He shook her.

"You are still sleeping?" he asked. "I thought you would have left for school by now."

"Jesus! What time is it?" Folake exclaimed.

"It's eleven minutes past nine," Jens replied, pointing at the wall clock. "Could you fix me something quick to eat, please? I'm kind of starving."

"Where is Auntie Sade? I called you both a thousand times last night but both your phones were permanently switched off!"

"I'll tell you all about it later. Please, I need to eat. I haven't really had any food since yesterday."

Despite being exhausted, Folake staggered her way into the kitchen. Her body ached. She knew she had already missed her first lecture for the day and another would be about to start. That meant two lectures missed out of the three scheduled for the day. She decided against going for the last one. That would give her time to rest more and take care of her domestic duties for the day.

Folake zapped the previous day's untouched supper for Jens. A few minutes later she placed a tray before Jens who was already seated at the dining table with his hands clasped behind his head while staring into the wall.

"Here is the food. It's fried rice."

Jens continued staring into space. Folake tapped him. "Here's your food."

"Sorry," Jens was startled.

"So, tell me what happened? Where were you and Madam last night?"

"Folake," Jens sighed. "I think I've lost my appetite."

"You've lost your appetite for the food? Or is it about telling me why you and Auntie Sade did not return home yesterday?"

"The food I mean."

"Are you okay? You asked that I get you food, that you haven't had anything to eat since yesterday and I've just brought you something. Now you talk of having lost your appetite without taking a spoonful. Talk to me, what's the problem? What's wrong with you?"

"Folake, nothing oh..."

"What do you mean by nothing when it's written all over you that all's not well? Jens, what's the matter?"

"Madam is dead."

"Madam! Which madam is dead?"

"Do you have any other madam? Auntie Sade is dead," Jens replied spilling the words right out and not holding back.

"Huh?"

"Yes. She died this morning."

"Ahhh!" Folake exclaimed and covered her mouth tight as though to strangle the screams building up inside her. "What happened?"

"*Shey*, you remember that yesterday, she told you not to bother yourself preparing lunch because she was would spend most of the day in a meeting?"

"Ehen," Folake said nodding curtly in affirmation.

"She slumped just before the meeting began and was rushed to Molee hospital. The people there couldn't attend her because they were under-staffed and under-equipped so she was referred to the teaching hospital. I was there until they told us this morning that she had passed away.

"Ewww!" Folake's scream finally found its way out. "Ah, Aunty Sade! You left this house alive-and-kicking yesterday! What kind of life is this? Death! How can you be so heartless? First it was the husband, now the wife too? Oh, those poor kids. I now know why I felt so uneasy yesterday."

"Folake, I'm lost. Life is cruel!"

"What will now become of us, and her children, those poor orphans?"

"I don't know o."

"So how long are we to remain in this house?"

"Folake, I beg you, stop asking questions which you know I don't have answers to. Please. You're upsetting me."

"Tell me why I should stop when life has chosen to make us feel hopeless again?"

***

Folasade's mother-in-law arrived with two of her children the following day. Ma Vero, as she was called, made it clear that she was around to see to her grandchildren's welfare and to secure the family's belongings. The week, two of Folasade's siblings also visited. They left after only one night. For Folasade's children – Damilola and Olumide, what they never prayed nor wished for had come and was in with them. They couldn't fathom how their mother whom they had been with during their school's visiting day some weeks ago, was no more and gone forever. They had suddenly become orphans, and they couldn't have been prepared for such a tragedy at this stage in their lives. They were however, left under the care of Ma Vero, their only surviving grandparent. She was the only one able to give them the comfort they needed.

Precisely two weeks after Folasade passed, Kehinde and some of JK Bank's top executives paid her family a condolence visit.

"...It was a black day for all of us at the bank," he said. "We witnessed our own sunset at dawn because she was one of our finest, an epitome of courage and excellence, a rare gem, a woman with a heart of gold. She was down to earth, loving and free-spirited...."

The COO talked endlessly, extolling Folasade's virtues. Deep down, he knew what triggered the heart attack the doctors said killed her. The autopsy ordered after the foul play revealed that she died of a natural heart failure. He had no doubt that Sade would have exposed him had her heart not failed her.

To show his sympathy, the COO offered a token to the family. It was the same amount he had offered her to look the other way. He was somewhat delighted that the family accepted the money. It relieved him of some of the guilt he carried.

"...I enjoin all of you to keep on with the legacies of this amazing woman. As for her children's education, I assure you that the management of JK Bank will see that they get the best. They'll be sponsored up to their first degrees at any institution of their choosing."

Chapter 11

It didn't take long for Jens and Folake to know that they were no longer needed in Venna Street. Their services in their late mistress' house were scarcely-needed, especially for Jens whose chauffeuring service was hardly called upon. Ma Vero soon complained about the wage bill even, even though her children sent her money regularly.

Ma Vero's did not have a steady income like Folasade, having been retired for two years. It didn't help matters that she was still pursuing her pension and gratuity for her thirty-five years of service to the nation.

Aside the cost of paying the two helps, Ma Vero simply didn't want them around as much. They reminded her too much of her daughter-in-law with whom she had fought an almost unending battle for control of the house after her son's passing. But Folasade had proven to be her match and more.

She was nothing like Folasade in her dealings with Jens and Folake. She was very touchy and often unreasonable in her expectations from the duo. She yelled at them over slight provocations and for the flimsy reasons. The house soon became a living hell for Jens and Folake.

It all got to a head on one morning. Jens had walked into the kitchen while Ma Vero bellowed at Folake over what she called 'terrible cooking'.

"This is unfair, ma," Jens blurted. He dropped the rake in his hand with which he was using in cleaning the compound that morning. You treat us like we are somehow at fault for the unfortunate turn of events in this house."

"Whose fault is it, then? Lazy man. Instead of showing gratitude for the free food and shelter you get here on a daily basis, you're running your mouth at me," Ma shouted at Jens. Her voice grew louder. "Do you know how much it costs me just to keep you here? No, come and kill me because it's my fault that you're in this condition."

Ma Vero seemed to always find fault in virtually everything, because she had her own opinions about everything, including how food should look or taste. Her latest complaint was about an apparent lack of salt in the *white* rice Folake had prepared for breakfast. It was the way she had always cooked it.

"Hmm! You are being too harsh, ma. That's not the way to treat people, especially those you know very little about."

"So you want to teach me how to run my own house, *abi*? Have you asked your colleague why she has never complained and..."

"No need to ask her. I already know," Jens cut her short. "She is simply fed up with your ill-treatment. I am too."

Jens walked out on her and went straight to his room. He began packing his things having felt that he had over-stayed his welcome in the household.

***

EVEN THE RICH BEG!

Two days later Jens moved out of the house to Jespa, a suburb on the outskirts of the city. He talked himself out of going to his former job at JK Bank. He knew that the bank would take him back because he had the goodwill of most of the top management staff. But it would be like going back to feast on his own vomit. It was the same reason that he had initially decided to stay at Mrs. Akinyemi's house after her death, even though he was getting little or no financial gain from the rather abrasive Ma Vero.

For the second time, he was to restart his life. A deluge of thoughts had passed through his mind before he finally made the decision to leave the house for the old woman. His first thought had been to abscond with his late mistress' car and sell it off. That would have given him something to start life anew with, for the second time.

Folake had spoken strongly against the idea after letting her in on it in a moment of weakness. She was right about the implications of his proposed action, which she also rightly noted might even blowback on her as an accomplice. So, all thanks to Folake, he was back to square one or almost.

He had a fairly substantial saving in the bank. He had started saving a year back at the prompting of Mrs. Akinyemi.

"Always save a little from your little for the rainy day which will come without warning," she had told him one day as he drove her to work. He had only succumbed to her advice after her third prompting.

Jens muttered a silent prayer of gratitude to her. If he hadn't listened to her, he would be at ground zero at the moment. He decided to use the money to set up a retail store for fancy male footwear. His rainy day had come, without warning, just as she had warned.

***

Folake became even more uncomfortable and unhappy in the house after Jens left. Things took a worse turn. Everything that could go wrong was wrong already. Ma Vero was livid every minute of the day as there was always something to complain about.

There was also the issue of unpaid wages which the granny never wanted to talk about. Mrs. Folasade had died just two days before paying their wages and Ma Vero had not paid anything in the two months she had spent in charge. That meant three months of unpaid wages.

Two weeks after Jens' departure, Folake packed her things as well. On the evening of that day she called her parents and told them she would return home the following day. No one contested her decision. It had been three consecutive months since they got the usual remittance of her pay for three months.

After the call, Folake told Ma Vero her parents wanted her to return home. She hinted that it was because of her unpaid wages, but the old woman just said 'okay' and went into her room.

As she left the house that morning, Folake felt empty inside. Her time living in it had impacted her so much that leaving it was tough. But she was also happy to become 'free' to focus on her studies, which was necessary now that she had just entered the penultimate semester of her academic sojourn. Failing any course would mean an extra year in school.

***

"Sister, welcome," Badmus greeted when Folake arrived home with her luggage – a leather box and a sack of books. He was seated with eyes fixed on his phone's screen when Folake walked in.

Folake drew a plastic chair and sat on it heaving a sigh. She was tired from bringing in her luggage all by herself after the *Keke* driver who brought her home dropped her off in front of their yard rode off. It had taken a lot of effort.

"Where's Ademola? He is at the school field playing football, *abi*? Folake asked Badmus, who seemed very much engrossed in his phone.

"No," Badmus replied. "Ademola went to church."

"Hmm, very unlike him." Folake remarked. "When did he repent?"

Ademola, just like their father disliked going to church; it was strange to hear that he was at church. Badmus told her that it was his newest girlfriend that convinced him to start attending church services.

"I was surprised when he got all dressed up for church and even grabbed a bible two Sundays ago. The same thing happened a week ago and today is no different."

"Like seriously! Thank God for him o. What of Maami? I haven't heard her voice?"

Her mother, who attended the earliest mass possible, would normally have returned to prepare the day's meal.

"They left early this morning to visit Jumoke in the hospital."

"They? Jumoke is in the hospital?" Folake asked, confused.

"Yes. Maami, Daddy, Auntie Kemi and Madam Gertrude, the woman that lives at Number 21."

"And what happened to Jumoke?"

"Auntie Kemi said that one of Jumoke's friends told her that Jumoke and her boyfriend were involved in an accident three weeks ago."

"Eiya! Jumoke," Folake said and sighed. "She must have sustained serious injuries to still be in the hospital after three weeks!"

"I see you brought back all your things. You're not returning to that house, are you?" Badmus asked after a brief silence.

"I'm not returning."

She was worried about Jumoke, who had over the years been like the sister she never had. She wondered why misfortune seemed to always befall all the people that were good to her.

Chapter 12

It was harmattan season and the morning was particularly frigid. Clad in singlet and a wrapper, Oga Festus was huddled in a small corner of the bed. He could see from the light streaming into the room from the holes in the roof that the day had begun, but he didn't want to get up from the bed.

The thought of taking a bath on such a morning had tormented him into wakefulness. Simply imagining the feel of cold water on his skin gave him the chills. But the scariest prospect was the face-offs that had ensued between himself and his clients whose jobs he had delayed

The house was virtually empty, except for Badmus. Folake had left for school and Ademola was at work. Madam Caro was off to see to the needs of her customers with Badmus expected to join her later.

Oga Festus was the only one in the house whose day had not begun. He lay on his bed tossing and turning. He was disturbed. Just then, Badmus walked into the room and informed him that Femi wanted to see him.

"Oh no!" Oga Festus exclaimed. "Tell him that I have already left for the shop."

Oga Festus panicked. Femi was one of his clients. He lived in the same neighbourhood. Femi's fabrics, which had been with Oga for nearly two months, were untouched. He had not done as much as cut the fabrics but had spent the generous advance he was given.

"But, I've already told him that you're home and still in bed," Badmus replied.

"Must everyone out there know our whereabouts? What if they are thieves or kidnappers, *nko*?" Oga Festus chided Badmus. "Go tell him I'll be with him soon."

Oga Festus stayed in the room for a few minutes after his son left. He thought of a believable excuse to present to Femi so that he can get more time. Nothing solid came to mind.

"Ah! Brother *mi*, you are here so early, good morning oh," he greeted when he finally stepped out to meet Femi. He offered his hand for a handshake.

Femi grunted a 'good morning' in reply.

"See eh, I'm done sewing that your cloth. It is just that the person I handed it to for tacking hasn't returned it yet and I'm yet to set my eyes on him for days now. Please, don't be offended. I will try and bring it to you before this week runs out."

He lied politely and expertly. Luck was definitely on Oga Festus's side that morning. The aggrieved customer was soon discharged with a false sense of expectance.

Femi was a man of few words and his reticent nature ensured that there was no altercation. He was being cajoled, but he let it slide, again. After a week of pestering the tailor, he eventually got his job, and what a terrible job it turned out to be – badly-sewn and unfit.

It wasn't that Oga Festus was bad at his job. Those who knew him in his heydays would testify to his excellent creations. His lackadaisical attitude to work only began a few years back after losing his entire savings to a Ponzi scheme, against the advice of his wife. Almost the same period, his previous shop, located in a tailoring hub that had a throng of competitors and even a lot more customers, was earmarked for demolition. He was ruined, irredeemably.

He had become increasingly careless and indolent after that. The reason he delivered a bad job to Femi was that he had misplaced the measurements that he had initially taken and forgotten the selected style. He had also rushed the dress after the customer threatened to bring *area boys* to trash his shop.

Miraculously, Femi didn't make trouble on receiving the horrific dress from his tailor. Customers like him were the type Oga Festus preferred. They respected his age and tolerated him. Others would berate him whenever he failed to deliver as promised. He did not like those ones.

Oga Festus' customer base had dwindled gradually since his new persona emerged. Even his own son Ademola, who he had hoped would take over his business someday eventually left and pitched his tent with his friend, Ninja, a popular welder who stayed in the same area he plied his tailoring trade.

Ninja, so named as a result of his injured left eye, was the best among his fellow craftsmen. His dedication to his work made him the number one choice of and endeared him to many, including his friend's son Ademola.

Perhaps Oga Festus's indolent attitude could also be due to the current location of his business. At the tailoring hub, before its demolition, there was stiff competition for customers and anyone with a bad record would be left behind. Then he was known as a master tailor who never disappointed. Things were okay financially then.

In his present location, Oga Festus had to endure low patronage and customers frequently defaulted on payment after service. He would have changed his profession, had he knowledge of any other trade. But he was a one-trade man. Tailoring was his life. He was stuck.

The downturn in fortune was swift and hard. Folake's income had helped a lot in saving the family, while also encouraging his indolence. With that income now gone, following her employer's untimely demise, the reality of poverty became even clearer for the family.

His wife had recently switched from trading perishable food condiments at Agbaja central market to vending already-cooked food under a small shed. It brought in more money, but it was far from enough. Badmus, who had just concluded his secondary education, was advised to suspend plans of continuing with tertiary education as there was no money to cater to it. It was however recommended, that he looked out for a craft and got himself engaged like his elder brother, at least, until things got better for the family financially.

***

Folake faced her academics with gusto. Her last year in school demanded of her more than she had expected, but she braved it, knowing it was her last chance to up her performance and redeem her grades.

She still found time at least twice a week to visit her friend Jumoke, who had moved in with her boyfriend cum fiancé, Kayode. They were both still recuperating. Kayode was confined to a wheelchair, having had his left leg amputated.

With both of them partially invalid, Folake helped them with as much chores as she could whenever she visited. Kayode would often tip her generously for the effort. This informal arrangement helped her sustain herself for the entirety of the semester.

Somehow, Folake was happy for the couple. The accident had sealed their bond rather than destroyed them. It was a blessing in disguise, especially for Jumoke, who had even before a priest's accentuation, already submitted herself to the 'I dos'. *The rain, instead of beating the eagle, ended up bathing it.*

Chapter 13

Sometimes, having things at one's disposal places them in danger of being devalued. It had only been a few months since Jens turned his back to the life of luxury in Venna Street, but he could swear a year had passed already. He still missed the house – Akinyemis, Folake, his job, everything. Adjusting to his new life had failed to erase his time there.

He missed Folake the most. While they were together in the house, she had never meant more than a sister to him. Well, she had also been his cook, he chuckled at the thought. He could almost taste her sumptuous dishes as he reclined in his bed. What he missed the most about was her frequent encouraging words that soothed him whenever he was distressed.

Being away from her for so long had opened him up to emotion he had never known existed. He had come to the realization that he wanted her to be more than just a sister to him.

He wanted to see her. He needed to see her. He decided to pay her a visit at the university the following day.

***

It was a few minutes before midday when Jens alighted from the *keke* at the school's main gate. He met a rowdy atmosphere. He soon learnt that a political rally was scheduled to hold for one of the city's Mayoral candidates that day.

Jens knew it would be hard to find Folake in such a melee. The thought was still in his mind when he sighted a girl whom he instantly recognized as a friend to Folake. She had visited them at Venna Street a couple of times and had even slept over once. He walked up to her and asked about Folake's whereabouts.

"I don't know *sha* but she might still be in class. You can check the 400 Level Business Administration Lecture Hall," she said before leaving to join a group of poster-carrying students.

Jens was slightly offended that the girl could leave him so abruptly without directing him to the said lecture hall. He managed to find his way there, asking for directions after every few meters.

Folake was just exiting the hall when he arrived. She saw him first. Students thronged out of the hall hurriedly. Most of them were headed to the rally venue where money would definitely be shared. A politician of Chief Martins' stature would definitely not make the mistake of holding a rally in the campus without greasing the student's hands.

"Hey! What are you doing here?" Folake asked when she finally found her way to Jens.

"To see you, of course," Jens replied.

They embraced awkwardly.

"This is not you o. This is not the Folake that I used to know. Since I lost my phone and your contact in the process, I had been waiting for your call but it never came through. It's not good oh."

"Don't take it that way, Jens. You wouldn't understand. It's been kind of tough for me," Folake replied as she led Jens down away from the lecture hall.

"Hmm! if you say so." Jens had a big smile on his face. "So tell me, how has it been with you and your studies?"

"Fine o. Just that the pressure is just too much now."

"Pressure *ke*?" he echoed, and Folake nodded her head in reply."Well, that's how it usually is. It gets tough whenever you're nearing the end. Just be strong. You're almost done."

"Yes I know, but you owe me your prayers."

"Sure, of course I do. What am I there for? If not to assist you in any way I can."

"Thank you." She stopped walking and faced him, "You are yet to tell me what brought you here. *Abi* you have finally decided to return to school?"

"Oh! Please, very far from that," he replied with a chuckle. "Let's talk over there."

Jens pointed to the student canteen.

"You can't be serious. Don't tell me that you left your place for here just to eat?"

The canteen was unusually empty, save for the waiters. Folake concluded that Chief Martins' rally was to blame.

"Folake, please sit down," Jens said. What will you eat?"

"You know I don't select food" Folake replied. "I'll eat whatever you're eating."

Jens smiled. He called on the waiter and ordered two plates of *ogbono* soup with assorted meat served with *amala* and two bottles of chilled malt drinks. He deliberately stressed the 'chilled' so that the waiter wouldn't bring them lukewarm drinks.

"So, how has it been with Jens and Jespa?" Folake asked teasingly as she moulded a bolus of *amala* in her palm.

"Jespa is not treating Jens well."

"How so?"

"That's actually one of the reasons I'm here. I wanted to ask you if you know of any viable business I can venture into."

"What's wrong with what you're doing now?"

Jens swallowed before answering.

"It's stagnated. I barely make enough sales to get by daily. The business is dying on me."

"Is it that you aren't saying the right words to potential customers or what?"

"It's not about saying the right words. It's about saying it to the right people. And the right people rarely show up."

"Hmm! That could be due to the location of the business? I know that Jespa doesn't have the kind of people that can patronize you. You will either have to sell what people there need or relocate your business altogether."

"What then is your advice?"

"It's up to you to decide which one you want to go for as you are the one with both the yam and the knife."

They went in silence for a few minutes. Jens pondered Folake's words as he ate.

"I wish to continue with the business," Jens said as he washed his hands. "It looks promising and I understand it well now."

"If that is the case, you really need a good location where people can appreciate what you have. You could try renting one of the shops in the school premises and continue your business here. I bet the students will be interested."

Jens nodded his head in agreement.

"The only thing is that it will be a seasonal affair as we students go on holidays regularly," she continued excitedly. "Even at that, it's much better than nothing at your place in Jespa. In any case, people coming into the University Park will compensate when students are absent. Add that to the fact that you'll be the only one selling such goods. It could be good."

Jens smiled all through Folake's lecture. He was convinced. No one had given him better advice since he started complaining about his business.

Thirty minutes later they were at the campus shuttle park where they would board cabs back to their respective destinations. Jens tried to slip some banknotes into Folake's handbag. She stopped him.

"You don't have to," Folake said quietly. "You've spent too much today already."

"No. Please take it," he replied still smiling. "Consider it a tip for your professional advice. It actually made a lot of sense to me and, to be honest, you've made my day. I truly appreciate."

"Oh! Come on, it's nothing."

Folake grudgingly collected the money and thanked him smiling. Then they both boarded separate taxis. Hers filled up first.

Jens was smiling as her taxi left.

Chapter 14

"If I had known it'd end that way, I wouldn't have wasted my time to queue up under that scorching sun that Saturday only to have the elections rigged for their candidate to emerge winner," one of the men sitting under the canopy at Madam Caro's open air restaurant said. The man, who was not addressing any of the other customers in the restaurant, was irate over the outcome of the recently concluded mayoral elections. His preferred candidate had lost.

"Wellington, you're wasting your energy over nothing," Gbenga, another customer replied through a mouthful of yam porridge. "You talk as if you don't know how elections are conducted over here. How can the mayor easily forget the system that brought him to power? The incumbents will always try to favour their own, most times, against the preference of the masses."

Wellington swallowed the rice in his mouth without chewing just so he could answer Gbenga who was seated next to him on the same table.

"Isn't that a call for anarchy? Isn't that madness? Do they think we're stupid?"

Wellington, like many of the clientele that frequented Madam Caro's *Mama-put*, was a civil servant. He had casted his vote conscientiously voter for Olabisi, a candidate he was convinced could bring about the needed reforms the city

Onyebuchi Obidimaru

needed. He was convinced that the election result announced after the polls was rigged.

Gbenga was a regular at the food shack. He ate his breakfast there every morning.

"The mayor promised a fair-and-square contest with no foul play," Wellington continued.

"Yes, he did that but you should know that our politicians only say such things to have their way," Gbenga countered. "In a way, he actually fulfilled the promise. Otherwise, how would you explain the fact that there were only three hundred and eighty-two votes difference between the winner and the runner-up? Doesn't it show that the election was keenly contested?"

Wellington was not the only person who believed that the election was rigged. It was popular opinion that the incumbent mayor of Goba had deliberately manipulated the election figures to deliver his preferred candidate, Rasheed, as the new mayor as a means of keeping a firm grip on the mayoral seat.

Most people had expected a victory for either Olabisi, the only female candidate, for her intellectual prowess or Chief Martins, for his generosity.

"While I cannot conclude that the election was rigged, I know that having a person like Rasheed as our mayor surely won't do us any good. He doesn't seem to have any policy direction," another patron chipped in.

The speaker was bald and chubby who sat alone at his table with a bowl of steaming Okra soup. He was waiting for his *amala* to be served and had been keenly listening to the conversation.

"Does it really matter?" Gbenga fired back. "Policy or no policy, do your thing the right way and you would give no chance for worry."

"No! It doesn't always work like that Oga," the man countered. "Don't you know that government policies always have a way of influencing the way people live their lives. They can shape, reshape or even impede businesses."

"Is that what you think?" Gbenga asked.

"That's the way it is," Wellington said. "That's why I stood by Olabisi. She showed that she knows our plight and has a plan to address them."

"Well, I don't think they can succeed in remoulding not to talk of impeding my own business," Gbenga quipped.

"Oga, are you sure?" The bald man asked. "What kind of business are you into *sef*?"

Gbenga declined to answer. How could he tell them that his stock in trade was hemp distribution? He rose from the table having finished his food and went over to the counter to meet Madam Caro for his bills.

"Today's meal was great," he said to her. "I can attest to the fact that my wife did justice to it."

Gbenga was referring to Folake. He had met her couple of times at the restaurant. He had immediately liked her homely demeanour. Since then he would joke endlessly about marrying her.

"Do send my warmest greetings to my wife. I would be coming for her soon," he said handing over a thousand naira note to Madam Caro. "Keep the change."

Madam Caro had dipped her hand into the pockets of her apron to give Gbenga his balance. It was almost a routine thing for him to leave his change for her. But each time he paid her, she would still attempt to give him his balance to avoid appearing impolite.

"Ahh! Thank you. God bless you *jare*," she replied with a smile. "That's the kind of people I like doing business with."

The customer who had been at the counter frowned. He knew the last part of the statement was directed at him. He owed her.

"*Wetin concern me* Madam Caro?" he said. "Abeg give me food *nah*. I've been here since."

"I hope you are going to pay today," Madam Caro replied with an eye roll.

"Bring me the food first. Even if I pay next year, won't it still go inside your purse?"

"See, just in case you haven't heard, a new government is in town o, and we don't know the kind of policies he will infest the city with. So your eat-today-and-pay-tomorrow has to stop. It's not going to be business as usual oh," she said as she dished out his order.

Madam Caro was bluffing. She knew people like him were needed to sustain her business. The coolers of food she cooked daily would not be sold if she were to insist on a pay-before-service policy. Most of those who ate on credit would eventually pay, even if it meant a delay until pay day. Fortunately for Madam Caro, her debtors were few.

Chapter 15

Jens followed Folake's advice to the letter. He moved his business away from Jespa. It had taken him a few weeks to make the move, because the prospect of starting anew was very daunting for him. It turned out to be the best decision he had made in a long while.

The business was up and running, and largely due to his steadfastness and determination, he was quick to reap the rewards. Just as Folake had predicted, there was a constant stream of customers, mostly young males. His turnover increased in multiples as his customers referred others to him.

Folake often dropped by his shop to see how he fared. It was often a brief affair. Their usual topics were business, school and family. Jens always looked forward to it, and would often try to make her stay longer than she intended.

On one of such visits, as Folake announced that she would be leaving and got up from her seat, Jens handed her a sealed brown envelope. He pressed it into her hand gently.

Folake gently felt the envelope to confirm her guess that it contained money. It was definitely money, and quite a substantial sum it seemed. She looked at him.

"What is in it?"

"You know it is money," Jens replied. "It is my contribution to your school project. I know you need it."

Folake had during her last visit mentioned her difficulty getting enough money to fund her compulsory final-year thesis. She had only casually mentioned it, but Jens had taken it to hear. He felt he owed her, being the brain behind the revival of his business. Aside that, he wanted to show that he genuinely cared for her.

"You don't have to give me the money because my parents have promised to give me the money I need next week," Folake said holding out the envelope. "I don't want my life to be a burden to anyone. Not to you or anyone else."

"Oh come on! I want you to keep it, even if you don't need it now. Sometime soon, you might need it," Jens voice quavered as it often did whenever he spoke in Folake's presence.

His affection for Folake had grown in leaps and bounds over the months since they left the Akinyemis'. He knew he ought to have been married at his age and he was convinced that Folake would be the perfect choice as a wife. Unfortunately, he had so far been unable to express that conviction to her.

He was afraid that she would reject his proposal down and that would make things awkward between them. He didn't want to ruin their budding friendship. Giving her money was the only he could express his affection without consequence.

"You should put this money back into your business. It is still growing. In any case…"

She stopped talking when a student entered the shop.

"Bye, see you soon, dear," Jens whispered.

He waved her off playfully and shifted his attention the customer who had already picked two shoes off the rack.

Folake stood by the doorway for a minute with a smile on her face. Jens had won the argument by leaving her with the envelope. She left the shop giggling to herself. The money would come in handy; she needed it since she was unsure about her parent providing it. For two days before the visit, her brother, Badmus was indicted for robbery and was in police detention switching the parents' attention, trying to save him from the predicament.

***

Ever since Badmus was advised by his parents to engage himself in a craft like his elder brother while he waited on them to gather the funds required for his enrolment in a university, he had ignored the advice and retired to the streets. He refused to accompany or help his parents in their respective businesses. He chose to loiter about the streets. There, he met his likes; those who had refused to work but wished for quick and easy cash. Worse still, he had let himself to be influenced by the bad company resulting to his unruly behaviour at home and away from it. He often returned home late at night, most times, reeking of marijuana and alcohol having lost sight of the fact that a sheep that mingles with dogs will surely eat faeces.

Even though his parents had noticed his new-found ill-mannered behaviour, they dismissed it as youthful exuberance, not realizing that their son was heading a slippery slope towards destruction.

Prior to the day he was taken into custody, four of his friends had stormed into a pharmacy and robbed it. They made away with the money the pharmacy gathered from sales that day, carted away some drugs and hijacked the phones and valuables of other customers who had been unlucky to have been shopping at the time. Luckily for the storekeeper, she was able to identify one of the boys as they had raided without masks. With that, she was able to identify the group that perpetrated the act.

She tipped off the police who swooped into action to arrest the members of the gang the following day. Badmus was yet to learn about the handiwork of his friends by the day he was arrested else, he too would have made himself scarce as they were already at large. Being affiliated with the gang opened him up to being indicted even though he didn't take part in the crime.

In a city where one is fined even for being right, what then should be expected when caught for wrongdoing? For the time Badmus was in police custody, he was open to different forms of extortions which fell on Oga Festus and Madam Caro's head. The money they had been struggling to gather together for his enrolment in school and for other expenses was expended while trying to secure his release. They couldn't afford to have him charged to court and punished for his waywardness. They were made to pay for all that the storekeeper said was damaged and all that was stolen from the pharmacy and the customers therein that evening.

Chapter 16

"Please don't blame me. I gave it my best shot. You know I did," Folake said.

Jens could see that Folake was visibly distraught as she spoke. They were seated in the courtyard of Folake's home a day after her convocation ceremony and she had just shown him her certificate. He could see that she knew he had hoped for better for her.

Jens felt sorry that he had missed her convocation. He had been suddenly forced to travel to the village on the request of his parents. They had sent a five-man delegate of uncles and cousins to him after becoming aware that he had been in the country for years.

It was during his month-long stay in the village that Erden Memorial University announced and held its convocation. He only learnt of the development the previous day on returning. That was the reason for his visit that morning. He wanted to congratulate Folake and also apologize for missing her graduation.

Folake told him she was glad that she was finally done with her studies at Erden Memorial University. She explained that to have successfully graduated, even though without the second-class-upper degree she had hoped for, was enough a victory in itself considering her circumstances.

He understood her. He knew how she had battled fiercely in her final semesters to salvage a second-class-upper degree. It made it even more pitiful that, despite all that, she only made a CPGA of 3.28, leaving her in the second-class-lower division.

Folake playfully told him that he should address her as a certified Business Administrator from that moment on. She added that he would have to pay her a handsome retainer for any future business advice. Considering of all the odds that had gone against her in the recent past, he concluded that Folake had a right to be thankful. They both laughed. Their laughter drew the attention of some of the tenants of the fifteen bedrooms apartment block.

They were seated in the courtyard because of the heat inside the house. There was no power in the area and hence, the room was dark and too warm. Folake had also chosen to host her guest outdoors so she could keep to her norm of not bringing male visitors into her parents' house, especially those who were strange to her parents.

"I wish you had managed to second class upper," he said.

"And you think I wanted less for myself? You think I went through all those struggles planning to fail, *abi*?" she retorted. "I am only accepting it because there is nothing I can do about it. God knows I tried my best."

"Hmmm! I know."

"If things had continued as they were before I went to work with the Akinyemis', I would have finished closer to First Class than Second Class

Onyebuchi Obidimaru

Upper. See, it is condition that caused my crayfish to turn up bent. I'm still proud of myself."

"Don't get me wrong. I'm proud of you too. I'm just worried that the result may negatively affect your chances of getting a nice paying job. It is the same certificate issue that made me resort to a security position and then a chauffeur when I was deported. I'm just worried for you."

Folake smiled when she saw the genuine concern in his eyes. It was somehow cute to see that her welfare bothered him that much. Her smile turned into a wide grin.

"Well, the deed can't be reversed. For now, I'm only staying focused and looking out for what next to do with my life," Folake said with a deep sigh.

There was a brief moment of silence. From where they sat, they could hear the occupants of the building going about their businesses. Someone was scolding a child in one of the apartments. Jens winced when he heard what he knew was the sound of a whip hitting the erring child.

"Em, Folake," Jens started. His voice was suddenly hoarse. "I want to come and see your parents about, *em*, about my feelings for you."

The last five words became an imaginary lump which had magically appeared in his throat. He swallowed hard several times to dislodge it.

"Your feelings? You want to see my parents about your feelings for me! So what do you want to tell them?" Folake pretended not to understand what he meant.

93

"I want to tell them that I want to marry you," Jens' confidence rose as he spoke. The lump in his throat had disappeared. "My parents want me to get a wife as soon as possible and there is no other woman I know that I would love to be with."

"Hmm!" Folake maintained her act. "I'm not sure I remember us ever dating or being engaged and here you are talking of marriage. Besides, someone has already come to ask for my hand in marriage."

Jens face was flushed when he heard that there was someone else. He felt stupid. How could he have expected that someone like Folake would not have other admirers? Or maybe for she had once said she wasn't in for relationship of any sort until after graduation to avoid distractions. Now coming in when he thought that the chain that hung around her neck with which she had used in barring herself had now been broken.

In the village, Jens parents' request for a wife and grandchildren had not surprised him at all. His father had made it clear to him that it was up to him to keep his lineage going as their only son. He had responded positively, mostly because he was convinced that Folake would be willing to marry him at short notice.

"It doesn't matter," Jens heard himself saying. "When can I come to see your parents?"

"How can you say it doesn't matter?" Folake replied timidly, her veil of feigned ignorance discarded.

It was true that someone had asked her parents for permission to marry her. The suitor in question was Gbenga, one of her mother's customers. Like Jens, he had never asked her out despite frequently acting nice to her. Unlike Jens however, Gbenga didn't appeal to her, even though he was better looking and seemed to have a lot of money to throw around.

Gbenga had visited the previous week with her mum's consent and formally declared his intention to marry her to Oga Festus and the rest of the family. Folake had however, decided to delay telling Jens because she knew he was interested in her. Besides, he might feel pressured to propose to her as well.

"Hmmm! So someone came and you are yet to tell me, *abi*?" Jens was angry. "So had it been I didn't bring this up, someone would've come behind me and snatch you away from me, *abi*?"

"Calm down."

"Calm down? I should calm down. No I won't, tell me why I should? Okay, even if you could say we never dated, could you not have told me as a friend?"

Folake could not find the right words so she remained silent.

"So that 'someone' who came is the right person for you, *abi*? Do you know how long I've cared for you, yet carrying myself like a gentleman around you? Do you remember when I first saw you lost in Venna Street? What about the period we were under one roof and I didn't disrespect you for once, waiting for the right time? Now you tell me 'someone' has come to snatch you away? Oh my God!"

95

"I'm sorry I didn't tell you."

"Don't be sorry because I am having none of this. It can't happen. I already told my parents I'm marrying you. See, you're everything I desire in a woman."

"Ahh! Take it easy," Folake said, realising that his voice was attracting the neighbours' attention. "People are hearing you."

"Even if someone had come for me and had seen my parents, does that mean that the person must marry me?"

"He might, if your parents so insist." He said, then realizing that she had just thrown him a lifeline, he asked, "Hope he hasn't paid your bride price yet?"

"No o, that would be too fast, *nah*."

"Then, I'm coming for you." Jens held her hands so passionately. "See, Folake, it's up to you to make the choice of the man you want as your husband. You know who I am. I'm very interested in having you as my wife. I can't stand or bear to lose you to another man, please."

Chapter 17

It didn't take long before Jens made the all-important visit to Oga Festus's household. Before his visit, Folake had tried her best to prepare her parents' minds, telling them as much as she could about him.

But his visit did not leave them as impressed as Gbenga's. Badmus and his mother were particularly clear that he did not meet the standards they had set for Folake's potential suitors. Badmus had often said in the past that her husband to be must be good looking, own his own business and have a good car. Jens failed in the car department, unlike Gbenga who visited in an SUV. The deal breaker for Badmus was that Jens failed to give him any money when leaving. His rival on the other hand had given him a thick wad of crisp notes.

A few days after Jen's visit, Oga Festus called his household together so they could collectively discuss on who to accept for Folake, his only daughter. He said he wanted the decision to be made by the entire family.

On the morning of the day the talk was to hold, Ademola received an impromptu invitation for a six-month training programme which was organised by a construction company for those with less than formal education, after which they could be retained as staff of the company if they performed well. He was invited for the training by Dayo, Ninja's friend who worked with the construction company. He had seen the mastery of tools Ademola exhibited in his craft when he came to visit his friend in the workshop. A slot had opened for him after one of the initially selected candidates got disqualified. The training was a once in a lifetime opportunity. Ademola had to leave immediately. So the family talk was held in his absence.

Badmus was the first to speak at the meeting. He made it clear that Gbenga was his choice.

"We don't want someone that will add to our poverty," he said. "That Jens guy is nothing but poverty waiting to swallow you up Folake and I am surprised you're willingly sacrificing yourself."

"You better shut up or leave here if you don't have any reasonable contribution to make. I didn't ask anyone to insult either of them," Oga Festus scolded his son. "You are busy insulting a young man who has got something up his sleeves and is seeking to settle down. You on the other hand, of what good have you been to the family? You only sleep, eat and cause us trouble."

"But my dear, is there anything wrong in a brother wanting the best for his only sister?" Mama Caro weighed in.

"Well, he can state his opinion without insulting anyone. I don't even expect him to have such opinion of anybody."

"I've already said my own oh," Badmus said. With that, he got up from his seat and left the house. He banged the door shut behind him.

"Do you see your stupid son? He just walked out on us as if I am not his father, as if I don't have a right to correct him," Oga Festus was furious.

"But Folake eh," Madam Caro said ignoring her husband's outburst. "With all your exposure and education, it is that man that you want for a husband? I thought school makes people wise."

"Ahh! Maami, what is wrong with the man I have chosen? I have known and stayed with Jens for not less than three years. I can say what he can and can't do, unlike the stranger you want to force on me because of money."

"It doesn't matter at all my dear. All I know is that Gbenga will make a better husband. He will take better care of you than your Jens."

Madam Caro was genuinely concerned about her daughter's welfare. To her, if her daughter could marry to a good rich man, the needs of the entire family would be taken care of. Marrying her to Gbenga would be a decision for the entire family, not just her.

"And Jens would make a bad one, *abi*? I know you're only saying this based on what your eyes see," Folake retorted.

It pained her that her mother's choice was solely based on financial considerations. It didn't surprise her, but it hurt still, especially when she remembered the sacrifices she had had to make for the family already.

"Is anyone even considering my happiness, or don't I deserve to be happy after all I've sacrificed for this family's welfare?" she asked. "I have no problem with Gbenga, Maami. But I am concerned about my happiness. All I want is someone who I can share my life with. Someone I understand and who understands me too. Maybe Gbenga will have all these qualities. Maybe he will not. Neither you nor I can tell. But I already know Jens, and he is just perfect for me."

Oga Festus had been quietly observing the exchange between mother and daughter with his arms crossed on his chest.

"Folake, it's not that we're trying to push you to marry Gbenga. No. I am your father. I will harm you. We are only concerned about your future and that of our unborn grandchildren – the kind of life they would have and the environment they would be exposed to. All these depend on your choice of man for marriage. But if you say Jens is your choice, it's your own cup of tea and it's left for you. All we are trying to do is to help you make the right choice, that's all."

"I appreciate that daddy," Folake countered. "I chose Jens because I can express my thoughts and feelings to him and he will always understand. In fact, he respects them. But I can't say the same for Gbenga who might act like he owns me because of his wea..."

"Folaaake, you are yet to even get to know Gbenga and you're saying all these things against him!" Madam Caro interjected.

"So, is it when I'm married to him that I will begin to know him? Would it not be too late then?"

"Well, it's all up to you Folake. You're the one to live with your man, not me, not your mother, not your brothers," Oga Festus paused for emphasis. "If the union turns out to be a blessing or it goes sour, it will be as a result of your decision. I advise you to take your time and think deeply about all that your mother and I have said to you today."

"I know, that's why I'm..," Folake started.

"*Oya,* the talk is over," Madam Caro cut her off. She hissed. "Tomorrow, you'll tell us what you make of the words we gave you."

Mama's Caro was angered by her daughter's refusal to accept her chosen suitor. She was convinced that Gbenga would be able to drag the family out of the financial problems threatening to swallow them. Realizing that she could not change Folake's mind was very frustrating for her.

Chapter 18

"By the authority vested in me by the church, I now pronounce you husband and wife. What God hath joined together, let no man or woman put asunder."

The officiating priest said these words solemnly to the delight of the beautifully-dressed couple before him. Jens wore a well-tailored black suit over a lilac coloured shirt and a black bowtie. His new wife looked heavenly in her white wedding gown. He faced, framed by the white veil was angelic. She looked taller than usual; thanks to the heeled shoe she wore.

The couple hugged each other and kissed passionately to the delight of the congregations. The priest had to make some jokes to remind Jens that a thousand eyes were watching them before he ended the kiss with a soft peck on his wife's temple.

It was a joyous day for both of them. They almost couldn't believe they were finally legally married, having had to overcome a lot of hurdles before finally walking down the aisle.

The journey to the aisle had been anything but smooth. Getting Gbenga out of the way had proven to be a mountainous task, especially as he had the bride's mother on his side.

Jens had eventually traced Gbenga down to his house for a 'man-to-man' conversation. Gbenga had greeted Jens' entreaties to get him to withdraw his interest in Folake with derision and arrogant dismissal, claiming that only he could provide the kind of lifestyle that a woman like Folake deserved.

"You're rich and many ladies out there will be dying to have you. But I can only get Folake, please allow me marry her," Jens had pleaded.

"It's like you don't get it," Gbenga had replied. "That's the more reason why I want to marry her, so that my eyes would be off these other ladies."

"But she doesn't love you. Even if you continue to pester her until next year, she still won't accept you."

"Well, it's up to her parents, not you. Now please leave before something happens to you."

Jens had left his rival's house feeling deflated. But as fate would have it, Gbenga was arrested by Drug Law Enforcement Commission (DLEC) officials that same day. His face was all over the news. Apparently he had ordered the killing of a rival drug peddler and the assassins had led the police to him. The police had then discovered a stash of various banned substances at his home and alerted DLEC. It had eventually become a very high profile case. Jens would learn later that some bigwigs managed to get him released and cleared of the charges against him.

Folake's parents had changed their opinion of Jens immediately Gbenga's true identity was exposed, paving way for actual marriage formalities to commence. Oga Festus had then invited Jens to bring his kith and kin for the traditional marriage rites.

His parents who had since been waiting for him to come home with good news wasted no time in accompanying him to the city. But providing all the items on the bridal list for the traditional marriage rites, proved to be yet again another hurdle.

It had soon become clear to Jens that Madam Caro was punishing him for causing them to lose Gbenga and the financial ease he would have brought them. It was particularly strange that the bridal items requested were extremely high, despite Folake's protests.

But he had proven himself man enough by meeting their demands, even though it severely depleted his resources and left him in unplanned debts. He and his bride had planned for a marriage without a party afterwards, but his mother-in-law's nagging left him with no choice but to solicit more funds from some friends for a low-key reception party.

As he walked back to his seat with his wife after the couples dance, Jens muttered a thankful prayer to God. In that same instant, his new wife was saying a prayer of her own.

Onyebuchi Obidimaru

Chapter 19

The wedding had come and gone. It left Jens feeling refreshed, as though his life had started all over again. The difference between this restart from the previous ones was that there was a companion by his side. With him and Folake, managing their new-found lives together, in spite of his rather depressed financial status, didn't prove as hard as he had feared.

In the quest for betterment of their household, Folake ventured into the corporate world to scout work opportunities. But her quest for employment on the strength of her Business Administration degree proved abortive. This lack of employment was not peculiar to her. The country's economic woes had affected the labour market greatly and most graduates, including those with far more impressive grades, suffered the same fate as Folake.

Most of the jobs advertised in the dailies, required people with years of experience on the job. Folake found this ridiculous to ask of a fresh graduate, especially in an economy where those who had graduated for years had failed to secure any meaningful employment.

The few jobs that did not require experience offered peanuts as pay while the ones with good pay were so keenly contested that only those with connections could land them.

It was during one of her job searches that Folake got to know of an opening for a position at JK Bank. She decided to give it a shot, with deflated optimism. The person who told her about the job openings said the bank was sacking a large number of staff over

105

large scale fraud. While researching before applying for the job, Folake read some newspaper articles about the bank. She learnt that some members of management had been arrested for defrauding the bank. According to one of the articles, the bank would have gone bankrupt but for the injection of funds by an unnamed investor who also authorized a sweep out of the top management team.

Most of Folake's past job applications had been turned down for her lack of experience and poor grades. So when she applied for the JK Bank job, she did it expecting the same result. There were many job interviews that she had attended without a result. As she had feared, the bank failed to reply after two weeks.

After more than six months of fruitless applications, Folake began working for her husband, serving mainly as an advisor. She helped him with book keeping and with time got his business registered with the Corporate Affairs Commission. She also opened a corporate bank account for the business. Together, they soon turned the fortunes of the business around due to Folake's managerial skills.

Their first three years as a couple could be likened to the two sides of a coin.

On one side of the coin, they lived a comfortable lifestyle. Jen's shoe business had dramatically evolved into a profit spinning venture that included four boutiques and three grocery stores in different parts of the city, tremendously improving their finance. They now lived in a beautiful three-bedroom bungalow in Drents District of Goba City. They had also recently acquired a four-wheel drive vehicle, their second car in as many years.

On the other side of the coin was the pair's unfortunate inability to have children. Their childlessness was often thrown into their face, even by people who were by far less fortunate. The joy of parenthood, the so-called fruits of matrimony, was evidently missing from their home. There were even speculations that they had given up their children for wealth and affluence. The dramatic turn of fortunes since their marriage had lent credence to this rumour.

Folake was often the target of the ridicule. She ignored the taunts and whispering, but wept her heart out every night. The problem would have been less difficult to bear had Madam Caro not turned herself into a constant pain over it. She would fuss over it during each of her too frequent visits to her daughter's home. She seemed to be marking the calendar on their behalf, much to Jens' chagrin. Even her daughter was tired of it.

Though Jens and Folake lived with spousal love, happiness and understanding, it was an undeniable fact that beneath the calm and contentment, they wanted more. They were not truly happy. Friends who married after they did already had babies. Having to attend the naming ceremonies of those friends' babies and birthday parties, without a child of their own, made it even more painful for them.

One Sunday evening, after a dinner of beans and *dodo*, the couple were watching a popular television series when Madam Caro entered the house without knocking. She took a few sips from the glass of fruit juice placed before her. After a while, she told Folake to excuse her so she could talk with her husband. Folake retreated to the kitchen wondering what her mother had to say that she couldn't be a part of.

"I have found someone who can help you," she said with excitement.

"What solution is there that we haven't tried?"

Jens' tone was dismissive. In search of solution, Jens and Folake had undergone series of medical check-ups. The results always showed that they were both medically fit to have children. They had also tried unorthodox medicine, drinking disgusting herbal concoctions, mostly at Madam Caro's instance, to no avail.

It was in the third year, that they resigned to their fate, hopeful and expectant that someday, something miraculous would happen, and the cry of their own biological baby would be heard in the house. But Folake did not stop praying. She often fasted and prayed every week, asking God to work a miracle in their lives so that all those who called them impotent and barren would have to eat their words.

So when Madam Caro said she could point them in the right direction, he had immediately feared it would have to be some spiritual nonsense.

"There is a herbalist…" Madam Caro started, pausing to gauge his reaction. "You know my friend, Iya Kemi, she said he is very potent. And his place is not far from here, near Dreps Avenue. I can take you there, let's try him. I really want to carry my grandchildren."

"To tell you the truth, Maami," Jens said, trying not to sound too dismissive, "we're tired of running here and there for nothing in the end. If there is a possibility that a child will come to us, which is our belief, it'll come. But as for running helter-skelter and getting cheated in the process, I don't think we'll ever consider that again."

"Hmm! Are you the one saying this?" Madam Caro was genuinely upset by his reaction.

"Yes ma. Of a truth, I'm no longer interested in any kind of help whatsoever from anyone. Like I said before, if the babies will come, they sure would."

"What do you mean you are not interested in getting help from outside in order to have your own kids? I was even trying to help you cover your shame and you are talking nonsense. Now I'm beginning to believe you are responsible for my daughter's childlessness."

"Hmm, Maami you have come again. I've always known it'll come to this someday."

"Why won't it come to this when you are not serious about your own problem?" she cried out. "This is also one of the reasons I disapproved of you getting married to my daughter initially. See, you know that if things remain as they are now, your people will start looking for another wife for you. They will displace my daughter who had done so much to make your life better. It is not a matter to be dismissed like that."

Jens shook his head. He knew Madam Caro was right about what Folake had done for him. It was also true what she said about his parents. Already his mother had hinted that the girl they wanted to marry for him was still available. But he also knew that no one could displace Folake in his life.

"Maami," he said calmly, "I really love my wife and I would never hurt her by taking another wife. In fact, I have bluntly rebuked people who advised me to take another wife in order to find out if Folake is indeed at fault for our childlessness."

"Oh, so they have started pushing you *sef*?"

Just then Folake entered the room hurriedly, disrupting the conversation. She didn't notice the mother's rage. For Jens, it was a welcome intrusion. He smiled as his wife changed the channel on the muted television and increased the volume.

"See the man you had wanted me to marry then, Maami, your 'benevolent' son-in-law," Folake said pointing to the television.

On the screen was a grainy mug-shot of Gbenga. The newscaster said he had beaten his wife to death in the presence of their three-month old baby. Instead of turning himself in to the police, he had cut her corpse into pieces, wrapped them up and attempted to dispose of it before local vigilante caught him.

"What does that have to do with what we are talking about?" Madam Caro was defiant. "Would you have been in this situation if you had listened?"

"*Maaaaami*! So you would have preferred to me to have a child and risk being killed! By the way, who told you my husband is the problem?"

"Will you shut up there!?"

"If you don't know, Folake and I are in this together," Jens said in a matter-of-fact manner. "You pay no mind to the fact that I'm also facing criticism from my own people for marrying your daughter against their wish."

"Why is it that you never cease to remind us of our problems?" Folake said, taking sides with her husband. "Back then, it used to be just me. Now it's both of us you want to criticise."

"You are only acting like children. But you both know I'm saying the truth and the truth always hurts," Madam Caro retorted. She picked up her bag and headed for the door. "And you, tell your husband to pass the information I gave him to you."

She closed the door behind her before anyone of them could say anything. The couple remained in their seats, dumbfounded by her outburst. She had spent less than thirty minutes in their house.

"Your mother is unbelievable!"

"I'm sorry, beloved," Folake said fiddling with her husband's overgrown moustache. "She is really a good woman expressing herself in a terrible way."

"Hmm, I hear you," Jens muttered, shaking his head in disapproval. He got up and went into the pantry. He had nothing to do there. He just wanted to be alone now that nature and its elements were conspiring against him

Chapter 20

Another year of childlessness passed. It was twelve months of constant nagging from both their parents. While Jen's parents threatened to bring in a new wife by force despite their son's unshakeable resolve not to acquiesce, Folake's family constantly nagged her. And so it happened that they gradually drifted away from their families, focusing instead on their business.

The year proved to be an even greater success than the previous years. They opened three more stores and expanded one of the older ones. Two more stores were in the works.

One day Jens was in the living room watching a football match between Arsenal and Aston Villa. Arsenal was losing by a lone goal and it was almost full time. As an Arsenal faithful, the score line annoyed him. He had been shouting at the players – the television actually.

Folake's voice reached him. She was shouting his name from inside their shared bedroom.

"What is it?" he asked irritably.

"Are we still going to the Akinyemis' today?" she asked.

"Ah, I forgot!" he replied. They had planned to pay their late boss' family a visit that day. Somehow the day's events had made them forget. "Yes we are still going… if you want to."

"We should go. We have postponed it too much already and today seems perfect."

"Okay then, I am ready whenever you are. These useless players have spoiled the match already anyway. Stupid Wenger!"

An hour later they arrived at Venna Street. They both felt some strange sense of guilt for not keeping in touch with their late mistress' kids, Damilola and Olumide. Even though they had often wondered how the kids were faring, they had never managed to actually visit them.

The visit turned out to be perfectly timed. The kids were super-excited to see their long lost caregivers. Damilola was as tall as Folake. Her brother was slightly taller and had some hair on his chin as well. They had grown so much, but Folake could still see the innocence in their eyes.

Ma Vero welcomed them with mixed feelings of guilt and happiness. She was pleasantly surprised however to learn that they were not only married, but visibly rich as well. After the initial awkwardness she opened up about the unfortunate turn of events. She said a number of misfortunes had befallen them over the years and things had become so bad that the children may have to drop out of school soon.

The couple were amazed when Ma Vero revealed that she had recently been informed by a financial institution that her daughter-in-law had taken an untraceable loan facility using the house as collateral not long before she passed away, meaning they could lose it soon. She also told them of how the new JK Bank management team summarily terminated her grandkids' scholarship in the wake of the investigation into the criminal activities in their organization. She painted a gloomy picture that left husband and wife teary-eyed.

Ma Vero said she had already talked with the principal of a nearby public school to admit them because her income could not accommodate the fee demands of any private school. The couple assured the old woman that they would help her as much as they could.

"It is only ideal that we reciprocate your mom's generosity and kindness to us," Folake said with tears in her eyes. She tightened her grip on her husband's arm as if seeking for confirmation. He nodded. "It is the least we can do, given the circumstance. You see, your mom was good to us. She treated us like an elder sister would and we cannot forget all she did for us during our time here. It is unfortunate that we lost her, but it takes nothing away from the fact that she gave us a home when all we needed was shelter."

As Folake sat beside her husband on the now-faded luxurious couch they once sat on as co-workers, she felt a rush of nostalgia. It felt like coming home with a lot of treasures after a long sojourn.

"I really wish we had known about all these problems earlier," Jens added. "We can't turn our backs to the predicament of the children of the woman who took us under her wings. We will sort out this present situation, and please don't ever hesitate to come to us anytime there is a need. We will always be here for you."

The visit lasted long into the night. Both the visitors and the hosts, especially the children whose faces beamed with smiles, were unwilling to end it. The atmosphere was warm and everyone was excited. Even Ma Vero seemed somewhat livelier. She thanked the couple for their kind gesture and apologised for the mistakes of the past.

The visit ended on a sour note however when Ma Vero asked them about their kids. Jen's response "God has not answered us yet" hit her hard. The truth of it and the casual way he said it, as though it were a normal thing, plunged the dagger of disappointed hope deeper into Folake's heart.

The old woman prayed for them as they entered their car. She prophesied that they would have good news by their next visit. Folake's heart warmed hopefully. But she was still sad and didn't talk the entire journey back home. She went straight to bed without talking to Jens who knew it was wise to leave her alone. He knew what the problem was.

Folake woke up some five hours later. It was almost three-thirty a.m. Her husband lay asleep on the other end of the large bed, snoring lightly. He looked peaceful.

At that moment she wondered if he was happy. She wondered if in his heart of hearts he blamed her for their childlessness. Perhaps, if he resented her and was only putting up with her because of her usefulness as a business partner. She wondered if he would have stayed with her if she were an ordinary housewife. A lot of thoughts ran through her mind. His dislike for her mother had become more unveiled in recent times. Would he extend the same hatred to her soon?

Folake suddenly felt an urge to pee. She got up from the bed and instead of going to the bathroom, her legs carried her to her dresser. Her hands too obviously had a will of their own, for they pulled open her drawer and picked a Pregnancy Test Strip. It was one of the two left from the bunch she had bought in panic a few months back.

Just as they had brought her to the dressed, Folake's feet carried her to the bathroom where, again against her intention, she found herself washing a bowl into which she emptied her bladder. She unwrapped the test strip and dipped it into the slightly orange urine. Six second later she took it out and sat on the toilet seat. She waited.

Some minutes later Folake looked at the strip and immediately snapped out of her reverie. There were two strips. Two strips! She screamed and jumped up. She ran into the room and almost crashed into Jens. He scream had woken him up.

"What happened?" he asked.

Folake ignored him. She ran to the dresser, picked the second test strip and ran back into the bathroom. She brushed her husband aside and dipped the unwrapped strip into the bowl of urine with shaky hands while her husband watched. She paced around as she waited for the lines to show. It was another two lines. She was pregnant!

Folake jumped into her husband's arms, he caught her still looking lost.

"I am pregnant," she cried. "I am pregnant!"

Chapter 21

"Yeeee! Arghh!" Folake shrieked. "Beloved, are you there? I think the baby is about to come."

Jens heard her from inside the bathroom and panicked. He was washing his face having just finished shaving. He rushed to his wife. The cry of a baby was finally going to be heard in their household

Jens had literally 'babysat' his wife from the third trimester of her pregnancy. He had left the business in the hands of his manager to personally care for her by himself. He even declined to hire a help, choosing instead to handle all the domestic affairs himself. He ensured his wife didn't lack anything through the period. He became her personal maid, cook, trainer and calendar, reminding her of her antenatal dates, her medication times and doses. Jens did all this to avoid any incident throughout the pregnancy.

As Jens grabbed the maternity bag already pre-packed for over a month, he prayed and hoped that his wife would be delivered of the baby without complications.

They had everything they would need to take care of the baby, thanks to his recent baby-shopping spree. He had bought several items, including some rather unnecessary things, in preparation for the child.

"Take it easy, dear," Jens said to Folake as he helped her get into the backseat of their newest SUVs. "We will be in the hospital in no time."

He drove through Ebre Road, the shortest route to the teaching hospital where Folake was registered. He met a human roadblock near the point where he would have merged into the main traffic. A masquerade was performing to the delight of a crowd frenzied by the loud drumming. The natives, dressed in flamboyant costumes, were celebrating the Gelede annual festival, held at the beginning of every farming season. The Gelede festival was a celebration of women and the power and authority of womanhood. Ironically, it had become an obstacle to his wife's expression of her womanhood.

Jens cursed as he made a quick U-turn with Masquerades and individuals in. He knew he wouldn't be allowed passage through that route no matter the explanation. He headed to Grates road, the longer alternative route to the hospital. His panic returned.

Grates road was also blocked. The revellers were everywhere it seemed. Traffic was congested, that, coupled with the terrible state of road made the journey hell. There was no alternative route. So Jens stayed on the route with other frustrated drivers, honking angrily and contesting small gaps to make progress through potholes, ditches and mud.

Residents of the area had complained ceaselessly about the bad state of the road to the appropriate authorities. Two newspapers had even done reports there after a nightmarish accident blocked traffic on the route for two full days. But the authorities only made it worse by digging on the few good spots just before the elections only to abandon the project after the polls. The rains turned the road into a cesspool of mud.

Folake grunted painfully after each bump. Each grunt felt like a knife stab in the guts for Jens. Jens cursed endlessly. He cursed the government. He cursed the people blocking the road and even cursed himself for not foreseeing the day's events.

Thankfully, Jens managed to plod through the mud to Ayodele Street and then back to the other end of Ebre Road. He linked to the expressway before hitting Hospital Road which eventually led him to the teaching hospital. By then Folake was too exhausted to make any sound. He drove right up the main hospital area and brought the car to a screeching halt.

"Help! Help!" Jens called out as he jumped out of the driver's seat. Two hospital attendant in white overalls emerged with a stretcher. Together they lifted Folake onto the stretcher and wheeled her into the maternity ward. Jens ran after them but was called back to remove his car to the park. Without saying a word, he threw his key towards one of the security officers.

"You can park it anywhere you like," he said before running after his wife.

One of the nurses collected Folake's card and the bag from him. She told him to wait in the small waiting area just outside the delivery room.

Unease gripped Jens. Each time a nurse exited the delivery room he would get up from his seat, expecting the good news.

Chapter 22

"Oga," Dr. Ronke tapped Jens on his shoulder.

Jens jumped to his feet startled. He had dozed off on the rather uncomfortable metal chairs with his head awkwardly rested on his knees.

He glanced towards the delivery room. A nurse walked out with bloody gloves. His heart skipped a beat. But he could hear baby cries coming from there as well.

"I presume you are the brother, sorry, I mean, husband to Folake?" the obstetrician asked Jens.

"Yes I am. How is she doing, Doctor?"

"Congratulations! Your wife has been delivered of twin boys."

"Ahh, thank God o," Jens said, going down on his knees and waving his hands up in reverence. His face was beaming with smile for his prayers had been doubly answered. "What about my wife? How is she doing? Can I go in now and see them?"

"No, sir. Sorry, you have to wait a little longer. We are not finished in there yet."

"Why is that? Is there anything else?"

"There was a minor complication but we will fix it and then you can come see all three of them."

"Hmm! What do you mean minor complication?" Jens queried. His smile had vanished into the thin air. "Is it that my boys are not alive or are they not physically okay? Tell me, what's the complication?"

"It's not something to get yourself worried about, sir. Your wife is experiencing postpartum haemorrhage, but, like I said, we are handling it."

"And what's that?"

"She's bleeding excessively and we are doing our best to arrest the situation. Put your mind to rest, sir. We're on it," Dr. Ronke reassured him. She patted him on his shoulder and returned to the delivery room.

Thirty minutes later they still had not given him any news about his wife's condition. He had seen male and female nurses going in and out of the ward. Unable to keep it together any longer, Jens barged into the ward. The question forming on his lips turned into a shriek.

Folake was there, motionless and lifeless with her midsection covered with a white drape. Two nurses held the twins in one corner of the room. The nurses were afraid that Jens would do something hurtful following his discovery. But he was too shocked to move. He just stood there by the door, glued to the flow.

Dr. Ronke walked over to him and held him. The male nurse in the room hovered around them, ready to take action in case Jens became violent. Another male nurse entered the ward.

"She lost a lot of blood. She didn't make it," Dr. Ronke said calmly.

"No! It can't be. It's not true!" he screamed.

"You have to be strong for your children," the doctor said. "They need you."

Jens pushed her aside gently and moved closer to his wife's corpse. She laid there lifeless. Tears trickled down his cheeks from his eyes. His grief was deep and palpable. He shook the corpse.

"Folake, who will take care of these boys you brought to life?"Jens lamented. "Misfortune brought us together and we survived many nights in darkness. Why must you leave now that the day has come with its light? Why? Why Folake?"

Feeling defeated, he sat on the floor. He mumbled incoherently to himself. One of the male nurses squatted beside him.

"Oga, take heart," he said. "Who knows what else could have happened? It could've been worse. She could've died with the babies. Instead, she chose to release them to you before leaving. Please take solace in them. They need you."

One of the nurses holding his children came closer. She held the baby towards him. Jens took the baby. He looked so fragile. It moved as a tear fell on its face. He asked for the second baby. The nurse handed him over. Another wail escaped his lips.

Jens' lamentations had attracted a small crowd of patients and staff. They gathered in the hallway whispering amongst each other while the bereaved man cried his heart out on the floor.

The nurses covered up Folake's corpse and proceeded to wheel her out of the ward. He didn't get up from where he sat on the floor with one baby in each arm.

"That's your mother being taken away," he said to them.

www.ingramcontent.com/pod-product-compliance
Lightning Source LLC
Chambersburg PA
CBHW061253170626
46809CB00007B/2969